Queer PAPI Porn

Gay Asian Erotica

Edited by
Joël Tan

Queer PAPI Porn

Gay Asian Erotica

Edited by
Joël Tan

Published in the United States by Cleis Press Inc., PO Box 14684, San Francisco, California 94114.
Printed in the United States.
Cover design: Scott Idleman
Cover Photograph: Melanie Friend
Text design: Frank Wiedemann
Logo art: Juana Alicia
First Edition.
10 9 8 7 6 5 4 3 2 1

Library of Congress Cataloging-in-Publication-Data

Queer PAPI porn : gay Asian erotica / edited by Joël Tan. -- 1st edition
p. cm.
ISBN 1-57344-038-8 (alk.paper)
1. Gay men--United States--Sexual behavior--Fiction. 2. Asian American gays--Sexual behavior--Fiction. 3. American Fiction--Asian American authors. 4. Gay men's writings, American. 5. Erotic stories, American. I. Tan, Joël, 1970-
PS648.H57 Q44 1998
813' .01083538'08664209045--ddc21 98-37740
CIP

Dedication

For James Edward Sakakura (October 1, 1959-August 12, 1996) and James Tan, my little brother: Strength, courage, and compassion, young brother, always.

Acknowledgments

Lots of people made this book happen, including Antonina Barraquiel, my mother and patron saint of queers; Geraldine Kudaka, sister/mother and mentor; and Napoleon Lustre, my manong and inspiration. Thanks also to: Krazy Kuya Phred, for making all things handy, practical, and electric happen; Jaime Cortez for the kind words and support; Glen Tuliau and Luna Francisco Angeles, for being sweet and gorgeous; Frédérique Delacoste, Felice Newman, and Don Weise of Cleis Press for taking a calculated risk; the contributors for their talent and hard work; and all my lovers and tricks who inspired me over the years.

Contents

Introduction

Queer PAPI Porn marks a milestone in gay literature: the first-ever collection of gay male erotica by Pilipinos, Asians, and Pacific Islanders. A sexy, smart, innovative book, *Queer PAPI Porn* stretches the boundaries of sex, race, and desire. If you are wanting vanilla with a dash of the orient, well, folks, this ain't it. In putting this collection together, I was amazed at how rich and spicy and edgy the pathos is in most of the stories. Like a rich, bubbling pot of menudo, this book is mouthwatering—but potentially dangerous.

Why PAPI? Not to be confused with the Spanish *papi-¿Ay Papi Chello, quien escribo el cheque?*—PAPI stands for Pilipinos, Asians, and Pacific Islanders. (*Pilipino* is the currently preferred spelling. Still, you'll find the authors of these stories have exercised all choices of spelling: *Filipino, Pilipino, Flip...*) Pilipino Asian Pacific Islander is a far more accurate description of a region that includes people living as far east (or west, depending upon your point of view) as Japan, as far west (or east) as India, north to the northernmost reaches of China, and south to New Zealand. Pilipinos and Pacific Islanders in particular often disappear in the oversimplified moniker of *Asian*—which typically assumes the experiences of East Asians, like Chinese, Japanese, and Korean.

So why fuck fiction? Historically, our identities as gay men of color have been either over-sexualized or made taboo. Given the racial stereotypes of Asian gay sexuality—that Asian gay men are feminine, physically diminutive, and submissive-it seems important to depict real, unsanitized, images of gay Pilipino, Asian, Pacific Islander sex. I want to wrap humanity—a body, a character, and a history—around the objects of *my* desire as a response to the racism in the gay community and the homophobia in our own ethnic communities.

Queer PAPI Porn presents sharp stroke lit, gayboy hip-hop porn with queer PAPIs as the central subjects of desire. Not all authors are of PAPI descent; nor are they exclusively male. Rather than further exhausting the strategy of compiling an anthology according to the identity of the contributors, *Queer PAPI Porn* is defined by desire. These are beautiful works of fiction, meant for stroking and provoking. While hardly the final word on queer PAPI sexuality and literature, what I offer here is a complex romp into the minds and desires of these authors of queer PAPI porn.

But enough talk. Let's fuck.

Oakland, California
September 1998

Mimesis

Virgil Vang

Not the language of words. Or the sound of wind. Even the music I loved I would banish to memory. I was losing my hearing at the age of twenty-seven. My universe of aural pleasure would soon be gone. Physicians, ear specialists, and psychologists could not help me.

While I could still hear out of my left ear, they gave me a battery of sensory-neural tests. At first, they thought that the stapes bone, which connected my inner and outer ears, might have exhibited abnormal growth, thus blocking the passage of sound. That they could correct by replacing it with metal or plastic. But they could find nothing physically wrong with my inner, middle, or outer ears that could be corrected through the usual microsurgical techniques.

My condition was diagnosed as psychogenic-a state of nonorganic deafness, usually associated with trauma or tension. I felt neither; indeed, I was the essence of calm. Lately, I had been feeling a peculiar lassitude, a disinclination to attach myself emotionally to anyone or anything other than my music. I didn't care to hear anything that detracted from my finely tuned sense of the world. As I recall, my last lover accused me of being insensitive to his psychosexual needs-but rather than listen to his angry stammering, or responding, I just stared silently through him, without hearing a word of what he was saying. That suited me fine, so long as he, and others, would just withdraw quietly from my life.

No one could predict just how long my condition would last. It could be months, or years. Learn the single-handed manual alphabet anyway, they advised me. Angered, I told them that that would be no better than masturbation. Then they suggested that I go through yet another set of expensive psychological tests at a famous deaf clinic in Palo Alto, in Northern California.

I did not take the tests. There was nothing wrong with me. No primal pain, no repressed energies—only, perhaps, a feeling of distance from ordinary people. As a precaution, though, I began to learn the manual alphabet, and to memorize my music: all the songs I'd written so far, and all the music that moved me. From bluegrass to chanting Tibetan nuns to Miles Davis to Stravinsky. The notes were in my head, sequentially—each bar, melody, and movement. I left the CD player on twenty-four hours a day until neighbors pounded on my apartment door and woke me up. Until the music simply got softer and softer. Until one day, it ceased to vibrate in my ears. By then, I knew how to use my hands to speak to others. I could read lips fairly well. But for me, sound had turned into a mute stranger. The key was lost, I told myself, as I drove across town to see my physician. I ached with sadness, for music was my life.

It was Dr. Philip Bergani who referred me to Mimesis. He had seen them perform once in Amsterdam, about five years ago. He thought that I would be a good candidate for the performance troupe, even though I was a composer, not an performer. He would personally contact Alain A., the director, since Mimesis would be in town to recruit for at least another week. Dr. Bergani would not elaborate; he only said that I would learn how to communicate in new ways. He asked me whether I wished to take the chance because the training was strenuous and risky. I had nothing to lose; I'd risk just about everything to hear again, I told him. "You will hear, you will speak—but not through your ears!" Dr. Bergani said. "You will learn a new language! Maybe even make music again!"

I drove twice around the block to find the small downtown space, 311 Mateo, located behind the Korean toy warehouse and a dumpster overflowing with crushed cardboard boxes stamped *Made in Taiwan*, or *Korea*, or *China*. I buzzed the code that I had been given. The steel gate admitted me to the unlocked studio door. I found myself in the midst of a vast space, perhaps a hundred feet deep by fifty feet wide, lit only by a spotlight.

In the middle of the painted concrete floor a bare-chested man was stretching. One arm reached down to his ankle, and the other was extended toward the air behind him. His head was shaved, and the spotlight caught his full lips, flattened nose, and high cheekbones. He was neither tall nor short. I guessed he was Alain A., the director.

He continued stretching, without appearing to notice or acknowledge me. As my eyes got used to the dim room, I sensed the presence of others. In opposite corners of the room were two other bare-chested men, also exercising. With a sweep of his narrow, brown eyes, Alain A. stopped and took in my face and body at one glance. I felt naked, though I was wearing a T-shirt, sweats, socks, and Birkenstocks. Gesticulating with his fingers, he welcomed me to Mimesis, day one. He wanted to see me by myself to ascertain whether I was right for the troupe, for what he wanted in a man. I gave him a capsule history of my composing songs for semi-classic and pop singers in Hollywood for the past ten years, and my dismay at losing my hearing.

Alain was about forty. Classic Southeast Asian features. More masculine than handsome. Wide-set eyes, sensual lips with a Malay cast, and a square jaw. He looked Filipino or Chinese. Or perhaps Southern Vietnamese depending on how the light hit his jawline and torso. His virile body reflected both light and darkness, mass and agility.

He wore black leggings that emphasized his muscular thighs and calves and nothing over his solid torso. I noticed the hefty bulge between his legs, and a delicate scar that wound its way up from his belly button to his left nipple. Calmly, he explained his background and his philosophy.

He was congenital—deaf from birth. But that hadn't stopped him from rising to a mid-level corporate job that he'd quit at age thirty-five. After investing successfully in Silicon Valley software, he had decided to devote the rest of his life to his passion. He founded Theatre Mimesis as therapy and expression for deaf gay men, and for other artists. Now his tapered fingers pointed to the red laser characters beamed onto the wall. Words appeared, the red letters glowing against the dullish concrete:

Embrace love and liberation
Your body mimics the universe

He signed: "We must search for metaphors of truth within the body and mind." Except for a soft spotlight on Alain's face, his body merged into the shadows. On the wall:

Each cell of skin, each atom of bone,
each drop of tear, semen, sweat, blood

New Age talk, I thought, almost as bad as the muzak. But before I could ruminate on it, I felt hands on my body, gently removing my clothing. As my eyes adapted to darkness, I recognized gloved hands attached to the arms of the bare-chested assistants. One man was white, and the other Filipino or Latino—the guys who, moments before, were exercising in the corners. Soon, I was butt-naked. They brought a small footstool for me to sit on. One held my head back as he shaved me, from my chin to my chest, splashing lime-scented water on my face and neck. Another kneeled at my crotch, and began lathering my pubic hair and scrotum. I did not feel awkward at all; I had nothing to lose. He shaved me until not a strand of hair remained. He motioned for me to kneel. Eager fingers parted my buttocks. They were lathering my behind, then they shaved it. As I continued to look at Alain, the spot went out. A few seconds later, I felt someone attach a rope around my balls and cock with a hangman's noose that could be tightened or loosened. The spot went on. Now Alain was naked, and I could see a rope around his cock and balls. His balls dangled low and heavy and his organ was immense, even when soft. His pubic hair was completely shaved. My eyes followed the trail of the rope. It led to mine.

Coil the rope of female energy within you

Alain stood still, breathing through his flared nostrils. "Breath is the essence. Follow me," he explained, his hands illuminated by the spotlight. He breathed. I began to inhale and exhale to his rhythm. As I breathed, feeling the breath circling inside my belly, the noose seemed to tighten around my balls and swelling cock. Alain began to move his belly, thigh, and calf muscles. He had absolute control of his body. The muscles under his skin flexed, tensed, and then uncoiled. On the wall:

Energy implodes within yourself

The image of a serpent coiled into three and a half circles, with its tail in its mouth, glowed red. Alain squatted and bent his head until his lips could touch the head of his own throbbing cock. Unloosen the knots, his fingers explained, as he sank slowly to the floor, relaxing his legs, belly, and shoulders. I did the same.

An assistant sauntered up to Alain, and began to run his fingers gently over his brow. At the same time, the other assistant laid his palm on my forehead. Downward, from the brow, I felt fingers circling my eyes, cheekbones, neck, throat, shoulders. Alain's face was completely relaxed; his eyes were closed. I closed mine and let the fingers massage each part of my body down to my toes. I felt a soft slap on my face. I opened my eyes. Luminous characters made the wall come alive:

We will breathe together 20,000 times a day

The assistants placed a silver ring modeled like a dragon over Alain's tool, twisting his balls through the ring. His organ, which had softened while we were massaged, sprang to life.

Taking a push-up position, he began to rotate his muscular torso on the ground. Using his thick-veined cock as a fulcrum, he spun a half-dozen times on his cockhead. Fixated, I simply stared. He must have tremendous strength-and ego-I thought to myself.

With his hands, he motioned for me to follow him. The rope wasn't long, so I had to follow his footsteps and twists and turns closely. Alain turned and bent over, spreading his muscular legs. He flexed his ass cheeks. The rope shortened until I was standing right behind him. I felt a tug on my ankles. I kneeled again. The assistant guided my head down, until my lips touched Alain's tawny, rounded buttocks. He spread his smooth cheeks wider. For a second, I hesitated. Then I slowly worked my way around the rim of his fuckhole, until my tongue found its mark. I felt him shudder with our mutual, silent pleasure.

Two hands swiveled my hips around, so that my back was toward him. I was being expertly guided to mimic the movements and desires of the master. The lighting changed with our dance, taking on red, blue, or white hues as we moved. He nestled his head on my butt, and I felt his teeth nibbling. My skin tingled. I felt the first stroke of his tongue probing the rim. Quickly, I shoved my ass up to his lips, wanting more of him inside me. But he was methodical in the way he took his pleasure, driving his tongue in and out of me as he wished, not to please me as much as to satisfy his own curiosity. I got soft.

Sensing this, he withdrew, got up, and walked away. Instantly, the space darkened. An assistant handed me an earthenware bowl steaming with the smell of strong-brewed ingredients, with the hint of anise, and other musky herbs. I drank the tonic greedily to regain my strength. I waited for Alain, but he did not appear again. The assistants indicated that the session was finished, that I should come back the day after tomorrow. When I stumbled out of the studio and into the street, the sky was already violet. I had no idea how much time had passed.

I spent the next day recuperating and trying to finish reading a love story set in colonial Vietnam by M. Duras. But I could not concentrate on the book, and switched to a novel on imaginary cities by I. Calvino. Fifty pages flew by without saying a thing to me. My mind was on Alain. He had awakened more than curiosity. In silence, he had spoken to me in a way no one had done before. He had touched something dormant within me, as only a sensuous melody had the power to do. Perhaps it was delayed reaction—the tonic finally taking effect. But I concluded it was purely psychological. His hands flashed in front of my eyes. Then images of his face, chest, shoulders, belly, butt, and thighs. I downed a shot of iced vodka and orange juice and went to bed earlier than usual, eager to find out what was in store for me the next day.

When the buzzer unlocked the warehouse gate to the studio, I walked into a transformed, brightly lit space. Alain was nowhere to be seen. Four naked men, all beautiful, were already stretching. I quickly stripped off my clothing, without any help this time. Gesturing and smiling, they quickly introduced themselves: Niyo, a lithe, tall youth from Japan; Vander, a pale, squarish dancer from Belgium; Solar-all smiles and round musculature-from Haiti; and Jorge, from El Salvador, a compact man with wavy hair down to his waist. And then there was me:

Virgil Vang, Chinese, with a quarter or so of Mexican blood from my maternal grandfather. I hailed from National City, right on the border between Tijuana and San Diego. What we had in common, of course, was that we could no longer hear, or never had-and that we were each distinctively handsome. We'd never be cloned or mistaken for anyone else. Another thing we soon shared: as the assistants began to bind our cocks and balls, roping us to each other, Alain suddenly appeared. Both ends of the long rope that tied the five of us to one another were tethered to his wrists, after being tied around his cock.

Forming the Mandala

We sat in a semicircle, facing the wall, as the red characters began to glow and reveal their message.

Make the Mandala
Rotate and rise, rise, rise

Alain undid the ropes from his wrists and lay prone, arms and legs outstretched. He began to rotate slowly on his buttocks. As he rotated, his cock rose slowly until it pointed toward the ceiling, its mushroom head filled with blood. The rest of us positioned ourselves in a circle around him, our cocks and balls still bound, as the two assistants went from man to man, stroking our thighs and genitals until we, too, pointed up. From the corner of my eye I glanced at the others: Alain had chosen us well, not only for size but also for shape. A thick dusky cock to my left, a tapered uncut organ to my right, and further across, two large throbbing tools rising from sets of smooth balls. The assistants guided us as we spread our legs, exposing our shaved assholes to Alain, who walked slowly around each of us, nudging and adjusting our positions with his blunt toes. As his big toe probed my hole, digging downward, it created a sensation and strange craving in me I could have never imagined before. I wanted his whole foot in me, his toes walking up my ass.

Revealing the Rose

On the ceiling, words appeared:

Revealing the rose, opening the bud

One by one we bent over, as the two assistants rubbed aromatic oil into our assholes. I groaned. With a covert glance, I saw the others stiffen with excitement. As we danced slowly around each other's rope-tied cocks, we began stroking each other, fondling balls and fingering asscracks. The assistants motioned us to walk on our hands and knees, in a circle. I imagined that we possessed the sleekness of a panther, leopard, horse, or tiger. The assistants took turns placing our cocks into their mouths, teasing us until we got hard. As we walked, or more accurately, crawled, Alain seized us up one by one. The rope jerked and I looked toward my left, where Alain was bent over, rimming Jorge's ass. I could not draw my eyes away from Alain's flushed, bulbous cockhead. Then Niyo slid under his legs, taking Alain's tool into his delicate mouth. But what I really wanted were Alain's muscular thighs around my waist, his thick cock pumping my hole. For that I would have to wait. But my ass was ready for Alain this time. I waited until Alain did Niyo.

Then it was my turn. I relaxed my buttocks and let him in. Suddenly, with a twist of the rope and of his body, Solar erupted in front of me, unable to hold himself. His dark cock expanded to twice its size as he shot, spewing droplets over me and on the concrete floor. He flushed and placed his palms together in mock apology. The assistants ignored him and motioned for us to keep moving in a circle.

As we moved, Alain moved in on us, rimming Vander and Solar by turns. What he found sensual did not necessarily fit the mode of airbrushed men in gay magazines. As he had joked earlier, all men were descended from the orangutan, from Maboko Island, Kenya, 15 million years ago. That we should not forget. He'd laughed, exposing his strong white teeth, one gold one in front.

Soaking the Stone

To quench our thirst and revitalize our bodies, we were given more of the same herbal brew to drink. The assistants moved a heavy wooden pallet into the middle of the room. Set onto the pallet was a dark gray stone, with a purple band around its upper circumference, resembling a lingam. I had never seen one as large-five feet tall and about a foot and a half in diameter.

One assistant took the end of Alain's rope and wrapped it around the base of the stone, anchoring it. The other assistant, standing on a ladder, doused the stone with rosewater. Alain walked around the lingam three times, placing a wreath of red roses around the base of the ritual stone. Then he kneeled, bending down and exposing his asshole to the rest of us. Under the spotlight we saw that he had somehow darkened the rim with an unguent or lip color. It was stained the same intense red as the flowers. Thus he revealed the rose to us, opening his bud.

Rising again, he began to stroke himself, at the same time dancing slowly around the stone, caressing it with every inch of his own massive tool and balls. His oiled oblong muscles curved with the curves of the stone. His dance became more frenzied, feverish, as he embraced the stone with outspread thighs and arms. Tongue poised between his lips, he licked the purple rim of the stone as if it were a butthole; below his belly, his cockslit oozed dark wet patterns on the rock. He was as removed as a dervish from the rest of us, who were staring at him in mounting excitement and disbelief.

Alain caressed the hard rock as if it were a lover, with more tenderness than he dared show to us. Arching his back, he came slowly over the purple band of the stone. The assistant motioned for us to follow one by one. First Niyo, then Solar, and Jorge. I was the last. By that time the stone glistened with semen, the air smelled of rosewater, sweat, and cum. My belly and thighs absorbed the heat of the soaked stone. I exploded. Wave after wave rose from the soles of my feet to my head.

It was a ritual of soaking the stone, Alain explained, as we sprawled in a sweating, nude semicircle around him and the lingam. He motioned for an assistant to untie Vander's balls and cock, and then ours. Smiling, Vander walked over to Alain, anticipating new pleasures. But without warning, Alain spun Vander around and brusquely began to shove his cock into Vander's ass, clutching on to his mop of blonde hair. Vander's mouth grimaced in surprise. Jorge began to tremble. Sweat poured from Niyo's brow; Solar averted his gaze. I looked toward Alain's large cock, as he pulled it, still dripping, out of Vander's ass.

Vander crawled back to the circle, blood dribbling down his leg. We dared not look at him. We were filled with a mixture of fear, humiliation, and desire. But one by one, we submitted to Alain. That was part of our initiation into the Theatre Mimesis. Finally, Alain pulled me toward him. I told myself to enjoy it, that this was what I really wanted. So it wasn't rape. By now I was too exhausted to know or care. He gripped my shoulders and began to thrust his pelvis against me, beads of sweat rolling off his body onto mine. His breath smelled of ginseng and herbs.

Our actual performances were not much different in substance, with some refinements, regional variations, and a taped musical score for the hearing audience. Alain asked me to compose something that utilized Indonesian xylophones and African percussion instruments, with a hint of the Japanese koto.

By that time I had rigged my synthesizer to my IBM computer. Though I could not hear what I wrote, I could control the electronic pattern of notes, scales, and melodies as they flashed on the colored screen. I plugged in the taped video performance and created an exotic score from virtual memory that only others, but not I, could hear. Though I could not hear a single note, yet, somehow, my body was still attuned to the vibrations that sound made through air. I could feel the blood pounding in my head. As Alain and I cued and reviewed the tape on the edit monitors—the close-ups of Niyo, Vander, Solar, Jorge, and me having sex with each other in the picture frame-we relived each image of the performance. Alain drew me down onto the editing room floor.

The digitized images flickered soundlessly by, casting light and shadow on the walls as we fumbled below the monitors. Our limbs were transformed seamlessly into silent film and electric shadows, wedded to virtual reality.

Theatre Mimesis performed for select audiences, at five hundred dollars per person. A hundred persons was the maximum for the hour and a half performance. Alain would rent large five- to seven-thousand-feet lofts from wealthy artists or patrons in New York, Chicago, Los Angeles, San Francisco. We also traveled to Amsterdam, Manila, Tokyo, and London for our performances. In each city, Alain had a stable of hand-trained local performers that he would add to the troupe, depending on the theme. Tickets were sold by referral only. We were sequestered and usually not permitted to meet our audiences after the show, though Alain usually joined them for supper or drinks later. I was the exception.

Alain said maintaining mystery was part of the Theatre Mimesis. Yet our mystery spread far and wide; men traveled cross-country to see our performances. (In the meantime, Vandar had dropped out, and Jorge had found himself a possessive lover who didn't permit him to work. Niyo regained his hearing, while Solar, lusty as ever, stayed on with me. We took on new performers, including a pre-op transsexual.) If members of the audience paid an extra thousand, we would, at the finale, incorporate them into the performance, stripping them naked, lashing their bodies to ours with rope and rotating them around the stone. A few got so excited that they licked our cum from the shining gray and purple stone; one man shot indiscreetly into the first-row audience, soiling their expensive Italian and Japanese designer threads.

In due time, Alain and I became lovers of sorts. I was twenty-nine. Alain was fifteen years older, but I was firmly in the grip of his dark psyche. I don't know whether you could call his affections anywhere close to love, at least as I knew it. His emotional makeup was another thing altogether; there was a strange pent-up energy emanating from his mind, communicated to me through his virile, silent body. His passion was authentic, as much as it was aesthetic and analytical. What we lost through lack of hearing we gained through the other senses. Because he was a superb mimic, he could intuitively draw out and perform the hidden desires of men, enacting our sensuality on stage.

I became Alain's man Friday. Besides composing electronic music scores, I trained new recruits and handled the household expenses and payroll for the troupe. Evenings, however, Alain usually made me wear a white jade cuff in two pieces attached to my neck with a silver clasp and chain that he controlled. It was decorative, yet cunningly designed. When he was in the mood we would go to dinner parties, and he would hook the cuff to a chain around his wrist. I would perform naked for the guests, sometimes having oral sex with them, while Alain sat, expressionless, on a couch or chair, wearing his custom-made Spanish sandals.

Only much later did I find out that Alain was charging even his close friends for these private sessions. When I confronted him one evening he just folded my fingers into my palm, shrugged his shoulders, and walked out to the bedroom balcony, taking his usual smoke. I ran out and dragged him in, pushing him onto the bed. I took off the jade neck-cuff and hooked it around his neck. He didn't resist; he smiled. Then I pummeled his still-handsome face-three, maybe four times with the same hand that I used to speak to, or caress him.

Once we got home from these dinner parties, you see, I would fuck him until we both came, ramming my cock up his ass the way he liked it, or I might rim his muscular ass at the foot of the bed. I remember that night I drove his ass crazy, until he stumbled naked to the balcony, as dawn began to lighten the rooftops below. He still wore the jade collar, with a disarmingly calm expression on his bruised face as he turned toward me. I had broken a tooth.

Over the years, what Alain had done superbly, I had begun to do better. I shaved my head and lifted weights. At fifty-five, Alain had lost musculature and was gaining too much weight. One day he simply asked me to replace him; later he would only attend final rehearsals. Finally, Alain became a voyeur at sex, even at home. I would find younger lovers from the troupe and bring them home. We would have sex in front of Alain, who liked to videotape the sessions with a camcorder hidden in one corner of a wall.

Now I was the same age as Alain had been when I first came to him that day in downtown Los Angeles. Though my hearing had partially returned, I kept that to myself. For my own reasons, I had decided to live my life as if I could not hear at all. The aura of silence suited me. Rather than seeing deafness as a disability, I had discovered that it led to my Self, my true nature, shorn of false words.

Strangely, I have no fear of the future, of the decay of my own body. But I hope that my art will live on in the bodies of men that I teach. I hope that they respond not to the raucous call of the world, but listen to the sexuality within themselves—*forming the mandala, revealing the rose, soaking the stone.* In this way, our silences will flower, season after season, in perfect mimesis.

Our Sunny Afternoon Together

Jay Ruben Dayrit

You and I meet like this...on one of those chilly days in the Castro, the sun casting one side of the street in a long shadow, thick as motor oil; the other side, blindingly bright. Men blinking in the harsh sunlight, dazed as if rudely awakened, peaceful dreams evaporating behind their eyelids. It's too cold to wear a tank top really, but I do anyway, catching myself in the windows of Twin Peaks, the bar at the corner of Castro and Market, my reflection rippling across the imperfections in the glass. Keeping their conversations seamless, the daddies at the bar in their Last Supper poses steal sidelong glances at me. I am sweet on their eyes, smooth like a skipping stone under their tongues and salty in all the right places.

I ease past the Castro Theatre. The smell of hot buttered popcorn spills out onto the sidewalk. Breeze past Take One Video. I look across the street, avoiding eye contact with the mustached man behind the counter. I owe them ten dollars for an overdue porno movie, but to hell with them and their apologetic smiles, like they're the ones who are sorry. Cash register ringing, making them rich off our small crimes. Irresponsible queens like me who forget to rewind the video, much less return the damn thing.

I duck into A Different Light Bookstore. The tranny behind the counter sings "Hello," bats her false eyelashes, tells me she loves my long black hair. "Giving girl realness," she says. "What conditioner?"

"Pantene," I say. "Don't hate me because I'm beautiful."

"Beauty always has a price, bitch," she says, then explains she has many a boyfriend, but there's always room for one more. She hands me a flier for her one-woman show, a performance piece called *Chicks with Dicks*. I fold it politely, slip it into the back pocket of my jeans.

On the table at the center of the store, there are stacks and stacks of current gay releases. A fiction anthology is prominently displayed at the front of the table. I have a story in this collection, a piece about my father. About how, as a child, I would watch him move about the piggery with a grace and strength I felt I would never develop. How my father always smelled sweet like ginger, how the sun never burned that smell off his shirts no matter how long they hung out to dry. How I wanted to run my hand down his bare back as he worked under the hood of our jeep, droplets of sweat gathering at my fingertips as I traced each vertebra down to the small of his back.

I pick up the anthology, feel its weight in my hands. Turning it over, I read my name, fifth alphabetically on the list of contributors, most of whom are unfamiliar to me, as I'm sure I am to them.

I run my finger across my name, as if it were written in Braille...for I have not yet gotten used to seeing my name in print. I feel a faint disbelief, really. Nonetheless, I am pleased.

In this moment of self-congratulation, I spot you across the table of books. Your forearms first, the way the dark hair wraps around the thick muscles, twists like a tornado down to your wrist, spreads across the top of your hand, and stops in a patch just before your pinkie. I want to reach across the table and touch you there, stroke the hairs the wrong way, feel their delicate resistance. I can tell, from your forearms alone, that you have a big dick.

I look up at your face and, to my disappointment, discover that you are much too good-looking for my taste, your mouth, nose, and jaw line reminiscent of the men who grace the covers of fitness magazines. Handsome, sporty, and a little too obsessed with sit-ups. I much prefer rugged men, men who don't count calories and can fix the toilet when it breaks.

So before you catch me looking at you, I make my way to the crowded back, to the shelves of porno magazines, their edges curled and oily from countless hands searching for something new amid the numbing sea of muscle queens and fuckable faces. I grab *OG Magazine*, not because I'm sticky rice—far from—but because I'm paranoid, paranoid I might discover nudie pictures of myself plastered across the glossy pages like maybe one day I was drugged, abducted, and forced to pose lavishly in some rice paddy just outside Manila. Surely that's what happened to these poor boys, asses high in the air, slanty eyes slantier than ever. Vietnamese, Filipino, Chinese, laid out like a menu.

You reach over my shoulder-your forearms are enough to identify you-and pull Jock from the shelf. Me with *Oriental Guy* and you with *Jock*; we might as well wear T-shirts that say *Flip* and *Honky*. You stand behind me, so close I can feel your body heat against my back. I move forward and turn slightly to look at you again. Perhaps I missed something.

Your eyelashes. They're what make you so handsome. Long and thick, they radiate from your eyes like a child's drawing of the sun, make you almost pretty.

I step over to the rack of postcards, all the while watching you. But you don't look up from the pages of *Jock*, don't even seem to notice that I have moved. I guess I was mistaken, misread your close proximity as something more than just reaching for a magazine in a crowded space. I find myself back at the display table, taken by a book on hermaphrodites. Inside there are medical photographs of the young patients before and after some doctor decided what sex they should be, solely based on the availability of tissue. Black bars conceal their eyes, protecting their identities.

Suddenly, you are next to me again, your hand brushing against my arm as you reach for the anthology. No mistaking that. Courage swells within me. Strange, for I am never the one who makes the first move, never the one with the opening line, particularly with someone as handsome as you. Rejection from the really hot is far worse than rejection from the just okay. But this opportunity, you holding the book, provides an opening I can't resist, as cheesy as it is. I reach out, turn the book over, and say, "That's me," pointing to my name. As soon as it comes out of my mouth, I regret saying it. You must now think me either a big fat liar or an egomaniac.

But you are genuinely impressed, I think. "Well, then," you say. "I have to buy it."

"Don't feel obliged."

"But then I can say I know the author when I show my friends."

"I only wrote one story."

"But it's the best one." You haven't even opened the book. I should be wary of your slick and easy charm, but instead, I let it play against my skin, soften my hesitation. You flip to the back of the book and read my bio, my life in five sentences.

"So, now that you know all about me," I say. "I'm at a disadvantage."

"What would you like to know?"

"How about your name, to start," I say.

"Well, let's find a book with *my* name on it." An answer so disarming, so charming I feel myself developing a crush on you, a small rush in my chest like too much caffeine. Together we search the books for your name. I pick out books by the most normal sounding authors.

I ask, "Michael. Is your name Michael?"

"Too ordinary."

"How about Fabio?"

"Too cheesy."

"Then what is your name?" I ask, already tired of guessing.

You look over the table once more before deciding that finding your name is hopeless. "Bob," you say. "My name is Bob."

Oh, that's not ordinary. But I don't say anything, being polite. You buy the anthology, and at your suggestion, we end up at Pasqua just around the corner. You get a hot chocolate, which is a likable order, unpretentious and sweet. I order chamomile tea, figuring it will calm me down. Flirting, cruising, picking up guys are not things I do easily.

You find us a table with three chairs, one next to you as you sit down and one across from you. I choose to sit across from you so I can watch you blow carefully on your hot chocolate, watch you lick whipped cream off your lips. "Why don't you sit down next to me," you suggest.

"Why? Won't that look strange, two people on one side of the table?"

"So our knees can touch," you say like there is nothing nefarious about us touching each other under the table, which, I guess, there isn't, now that you phrase it so innocently.

When I switch chairs, you scoot closer to me, lean your head next to my ear like you are about to tell me a secret. I feel the warmth of your breath on my neck. You place the anthology on the table. "So, what do you write about?" you ask softly like we are on the phone and you want to know what I am wearing. A pedestrian question to which there is never a unique answer. I consider which stock answer to give you, which one will impress you, entice you. I wait long enough for you to believe you are the first to ever ask this question. "I try to tell the truth, even if it *is* fiction," I say, placing my hand on the book, suddenly self-conscious.

"Do you ever write about sex?" you ask, putting your finger on my thumbnail.

"Um, what are you doing?"

"See," you say. "Now, we're holding hands."

"You can do it for real, if you'd like. I don't mind."

You take my hand into yours, enclose it completely in your cupped palms. Your fingers are strong and angular, the hands of an architect or a surgeon.

"So, what do you do?" I ask, avoiding the sex question.

"I'm an engineer."

"Civil, mechanical...genetic?"

"Nautical.... I design ship engines for oil tankers. Combustion systems and propellers mostly."

I imagine what you might do every day. I see you standing under a ship in dry dock, below an enormous propeller the size of a house, blades gently curved as if bent by the wind. You are wearing a hard hat, inspecting your design, a creation that will propel this ship across endless oceans, over swells formed in distant storms, slowly and reliably, carrying a crew of five, who bring aboard paperbacks and watercolors to keep them company. How romantic a life it must be. I wonder if you are that type, the kind of person who would be happy with such a solitary life.

"So, tell me something interesting about oil tankers," I say.

"Well, let's see. During an oil spill, your priorities are the crew first. Make sure there's no loss of human life. The ship is second, 'cause they cost about ten million dollars, and the environment is last, unfortunately."

Not the romantic answer I expected, but still, I appreciate your honesty. You take hold of my thigh, turning me toward you, and place my knee between your legs. I slide myself closer, easing my knee into your crotch, gently nudging against your balls. This happens naturally. We fit together, neighboring pieces in a jigsaw puzzle. You examine my hand, tracing the thin veins along my wrist. "I like this," you say softly.

"What, my veins...or being together like this?"

"Both."

"Me too," I say.

Wisps of chest hair peek out from under your collar just below your Adam's apple. I wonder how thickly it grows there, in what kind of pattern—a diamond or large swirls that sweep over your pecs?

"I like your hands," you say. "They're long like a musician's, but still masculine."

"They're my father's hands. He raises pigs. The older I get, the more I look like him. It's kinda weird."

"Will you sign my book?" you ask.

"Oh god...what will I write?"

"I don't know. Think of something," you say and turn to the first page of my story. You hold the book open on the table.

"I don't have a pen," I say.

"I'll get one from the counter." As you get up, I struggle to find something to write, something that doesn't sound stupid or glib. You come back and hand me the pen. I feel you looking at me as I hold it over the page. After careful consideration, I finally write, *Bob, Always tell the truth.* And then I sign it.

"Put down your phone number," you insist.

I jot down my work number. "There," I say. "Give me yours." I pull out the *Chicks with Dicks* flier and hand it to you. You write two phone numbers. One has a little *w* beside it, the other an *h.* Your penmanship is consistent and legible. Must have been all the years in engineering school, drafting up plans other people must follow.

"So, I have to ask you, Bob," I say. You look at me expectantly, your eyes attentive. "Are you in a relationship?"

You look down to the floor and say, "No." I cannot imagine why someone with your charm, your looks—your butch job-would not be in a relationship.

"Well, I am," I confess. Always tell the truth. You sit back in your chair. I feel you pull away, the way waves pull away from the beach, leaving the sand smooth and untouched. I want you close to me, so that I can smell the sweet chocolate on your breath, feel your body heat again. I don't blame you though. I've led you on. "Are you disappointed?" I ask. If you will not put my hand into yours again, I need at least that flattery, your disappointment.

"Yes...but I have no right to be. I have a boyfriend, too."

"So you lied to me," I say, feigning anger.

"Oh, no. Our first lovers' quarrel," you joke. "I just didn't want to let you down." Somehow, now, you seem more real, not suave and polished, your face not as perfectly handsome. I notice the pores on your nose and the soft fuzz on your earlobes that will grow thick and wiry as you age.

"Do you love him?" you ask me. "Your boyfriend."

"Yes...very much so."

"I was enjoying this so much though," you sigh. "I was enjoying...pretending that we are on a first date or something. It's kind of exciting and new. I don't know. I guess I like to flirt. My boyfriend gets so fuckin' jealous though. It's like he's insane."

"Vietnamese?" I ask.

"How'd you know?"

"They're the jealous ones."

You tell me that you've been with Thu for a little over a year. You live together in a small house in Berkeley. He is a waiter at a Thai restaurant, goes to community college in Oakland, has been in America for only two years. I struggle to suppress my laughter. But what you tell me next disturbs me. You pay for everything: rent, food, long-distance phone calls to Vietnam. You recently bought him a Leica camera and a two-thousand-dollar mountain bike simply because he asked for them. When you suggested he look at cheaper ones, he accused you of denying him the American dream.

I think to myself, Oh...my...god. You are the Great White Hope of sugar daddies, and he has you wrapped like cotton candy around his greedy little chopsticks. How can I still find you attractive? But I do, irresistibly so. I thought I was better than this.

"What's your boyfriend's name?" you ask.

"David. He's a sweet man. I'm lucky." And that is all I decide to tell you, afraid to disclose too much, as you have already. And then suddenly, here we are in a coffee shop in the Castro, both of us in relationships. We have reached an impasse, like two bottoms in bed. "What do we do now?" I ask.

"I don't know. What would you like to do?"

I almost suggest getting a room at Beck's Motor Lodge, a ten-minute walk up the street, but I wouldn't want you to find me so cheap and tawdry. "I should go home," I say, hoping that you might suggest the Motor Lodge yourself.

"I should head home too," you say. Damn.

We walk up the street to where the F-Line circles back onto Market. On the way up Castro, our hands bump and you take hold of mine. Other men hurry past us, on their way to dinner, to buy flowers, to gay AA meetings, going about their lives, hardly giving us a second thought. For all they know, we've been together for years, share a flat by Duboce Park and have a joint checking account. Little do they know we are both being unfaithful.

On the trolley, we say little of relevance. You mention how the days have gotten noticeably shorter, how that always makes you sad. You hold my hand on your lap, the way a high school girl might hold the hand of her boyfriend, such a contradiction to the way you look, your thick forearms, your strong hands, your masculine frame. Occasionally, you look at me and smile, which I wish you wouldn't do now. Already I know your smile only makes it harder to say good-bye.

At the Civic Center subway station, you ride the escalator with me down to the MUNI platform, though you take BART home. "You don't need to wait with me," I say.

"But I want to."

I find myself struggling for something to say, searching randomly the way we looked for your name on a book in the bookstore. I want to tell you how badly I want to see you again, that I want you to call me, to put your arms around me so I can bury my face in the slope of your neck and take in the smell of the shipyard, the smell of engine fuel and welded steel. But I know I can't tell you any of this without my voice faltering, succumbing to desperation.

The platform is empty save for three black kids hanging out at the bottom of the escalator, listening to rap music on a little boom box. They know all the lyrics and rap along with a cool indifference. We walk to the other end of the platform. I look down the tunnel, because I don't want to look at you, afraid I might memorize your face, have something to miss once you are gone.

You put your arms around me, turn me so we are facing each other. "Bob," I say, protesting just a little.

"I've wanted to do this ever since I saw you in the bookstore, showing off your body like that, wearing your little tank top," you say, mouth so close to mine we are almost kissing. I am suddenly embarrassed by my obvious vanity, my transparent motivations. You pull me closer, kiss me on the neck, your lips parted, the hard edge of your teeth against my skin.

"What about those kids down there," I whisper into your ear.

"It's San Francisco. They should be used to it," you say and kiss the other side of my neck. You circle around me and walk me backwards until we are both hidden behind the big column in the middle of the platform. With my back against the marble, I feel the cold seep through my tank top like rain. You brush your lips against my cheek, moving toward my mouth. I feel the soft stubble of your chin scrape my jaw. When I move to kiss you, you pull away, smiling. Your crotch presses against mine. I can feel your dick getting hard. You reach into your pocket, adjust it so that it rests alongside your hip. I look down and see that I guessed right the first time I saw you. The thick bulge extends just beyond your hip, constrained only by the material of your khakis.

You pull my tank top up across my chest. "Nice," you whisper, running your hands along my abs. "Very nice." You crouch down, keeping your dick pressed against my thigh. You wet my nipple with a single broad stroke of your tongue, circle it before biting down. I grab the back of your head and press your face against my chest. You lift my arms over my head and lick the side of my chest until your face is in my armpit. You breathe in deeply, saying, "God, you smell so fuckin' good."

You undo the top button of your khakis and guide my hand down into your boxers. "Jerk me off," you whisper and kiss me, forcing my mouth open with your tongue. I can smell myself on your lips. I grab hold of your dick, barely able to wrap my fingers around it, feel your hard stomach and soft pubic hair against the top of my hand as I stroke you off.

Taking my other hand, you slip it up under your shirt and say,

"Yeah...pinch my nipple." I pinch it. "Hard," you say. "I like it hard. Make it hurt."

I take your nipple between the knuckle of my index finger and the nail of my thumb and clamp down on it. "Yes," trails from your mouth like a snake. "Twist it," you say. I twist so hard my forearm shakes. My other hand strokes your dick, feeling it stiffen in my hand. "Harder," you moan, and I squeeze your nipple so hard my arm aches. Your mouth falls open. Your pupils roll back behind your fluttering eyelids, and I watch you sail away like one of your ships, to the first time someone ever did this to you. Who was it? Was it your college roommate, a soccer player maybe who liked to get drunk, fool around and then, in the morning, blame it on the beer? Or was it earlier than that? Maybe it was your girlfriend back when you thought you were straight. Or maybe it was the kid who moved into your neighborhood the summer before eighth grade. Was it up in the tree house your father built, the stars scattered overhead, crickets singing in the long blades of grass at the trunk of the tree where the lawn mower couldn't reach?

A three-car train rushes by in a rumbling blur. In my periphery, I catch a glimpse of an old Chinese lady looking out the window. The train grinds to a halt at the other end of the platform, just out of range so that the passengers in the last car can't see us. You are oblivious to the passing trains, to the people that might have seen us, to the black kids who are now boarding, their music now muffled, and I suspect, oblivious to me as you cum, unloading hot sperm into your boxers with each stroke of my hand.

Feeling your cum in my hand and your hip thrusting against

my crotch, I cum too. I cum quietly, without touching myself, without even so much as a gasp for air. You collapse into me. The weight of your body presses me against the marble column. Another train rolls by, this time going the other way, gaining momentum before rushing down the tunnel.

I don't know how long we stay this way, leaning into each other, catching our breath. Long enough for your cum to grow cold in my hand...and long enough for me to realize that you will never call me and I will never call you.

I want to believe that you don't call because Thu finds my phone number in the anthology. He rips out the page in a jealous fit, burns it over the blue flame of the gas stove, ashes settling like black feathers on the clean linoleum floor. I want to believe this if only to protect my ego.

And I will never call you, because when I get home tonight, I will throw my jeans into the wash before David notices the dried cum behind the knee where I wiped my hand after I let go of you. When I take my jeans out of the drier, the flier has been washed and dried into an unrecognizable ball of yellow pulp. Strangely enough, I will be relieved that your phone number has been rendered illegible, all evidence washed away.

So you will never call me, and I will never call you. Weeks, months, and, eventually, years will pass, and we will forget about each other...except for maybe when I see oil tankers pass below the Golden Gate Bridge or when you meet someone who fancies himself a writer; then we might think of each other. But for the most part, our sunny afternoon together will grow increasingly anecdotal and irrelevant, nothing compared to my life with David, your life with Thu. I suspect we knew this all along.

It's San Francisco. We should be used to these things.

I ease out from under you, wipe my hand behind my knee. "I should get going," I say.

"Yeah, me too. I'll call you, though," you say, going through the formalities.

"We should have lunch sometime." I do the same.

"That'll be cool." You are walking backward now, tucking in your shirt. "I'll catch up with you later."

"Bye," I say and watch you ride the escalator away from me. One last wave, and you are gone. And I am alone on the platform, waiting for the M-Ocean View to take me home.

Continence

Jaime Cortez

I

My first forty lovers were Japanese. I met them by night on park trails where they padded about with animal caution, keeping to the shadows and passing briskly through pools of streetlight. At times, only the glowing tips of cigarettes marked their presence in the dark. The taste of smoke on a man's tongue remains the essential flavor of sex to me.

II

From the teachers' room window, I watched the horseplay of the Nishikawa High School baseball team. A crushing defeat in the Yamanashi Prefectural tournament had resulted in a collective head-shaving of atonement. They squatted about the dugout in the flat-footed style of Japanese men, their denuded heads bobbing as they wolfed down their bento. They were the roughest, most physical boys in school, constantly grabbing, pinching and pushing each other. Theirs was a fiercely boyish world, centered around ball and their teammates. Girls were never seen in their area of the schoolyard, but the team did not lack for schoolmates to dominate. A rigid hierarchy circumscribed their every interaction. At noon, the junior members of the team scampered to the lunchroom and the neighboring grocery stores to bring lunch, soda, and candy to the upperclassmen.

The older boys appeared to have license to do as they wished with their underlings. They had particular favorites, whom they pulled down onto their laps, wrapping their arms around their waists. They sat like this, in groups of three or four couples, chatting idly in the September sun. At times, the younger boys sat on the bleachers behind the seniors, massaging the prickly stubble of their scalps and necks with play-callused fingers.

Turning away from the dugout, I watched the cool physical continence of the adult male teachers, who touched each other only during the red-faced euphoria of sporting coups and in the slushy depths of drunkenness.

I watched sixteen-year-old Mitsui Kun and Imamura Kun walk hand-in-hand to homeroom. In my best unwitting gaigin voice, I opened a discussion on queerness. "Umm, Suruki Sensei, those boys are holding hands. In America, usually it is only gay men who hold hands. Are they gay boys?" Suruki Sensei blushed at my impertinent question, and responded with embarrassed head shaking. "No, no, no, they are not homosexual boys. They are friends. We Japanese hold hands in school...sometimes. Maybe there are no homosexuals in Japan." Suruki assured me of this as a parent might assure a child that there are no monsters under the bed. He turned sheepishly to Vice-Principal Kawakami and translated my question. A wave of giggles and nervous smiles spread through the teachers' room. Kawakami said something incomprehensible and everyone laughed uproariously. The only words I could make out were "San Francisco."

With his tiny, fluttery hands, lilting speech, and badly dyed hair, Vice-Principal Kawakami had always seemed to me the epitome of an old queen. Shamelessly sycophantic, he used outrageously florid speech patterns as he kissed the principal's ass, stuffing a dizzying array of honorifics into every open space in his sentences. For staff meetings, he favored powder blue terry slippers. The slippers featured an embroidered playboy bunny with a bow on its head. No one else seemed to think it was high comedy to watch Kawakami cross his legs at the knee, and nervously bounce his playgirl slippers. My newness in Japan made it almost impossible to recalibrate my incipient gaydar and determine if Kawakami's behaviors fell within the acceptable range of Japanese maleness. I could only smirk in comic isolation and wonder if what I was seeing was strange or not. My teachers' room embarrassment only heightened my need to find other queers. I embarked upon a threefold plan of action: Shut my mouth. Open my eyes and ears. Find queers.

III

I am tempted to say I discovered Suriyoru Park and anonymous sex accidentally, but that explanation is incomplete. I was twenty-two, with the sex drive appropriate to that age. My body was demanding sex, and an appallingly large percentage of my brain and five senses were working full-time toward that end.

Late one night, I bicycled home through a pleasant haze of vodka. As I waited for the streetlight to turn, I noted a furtive young man making his way up the trail that lead to Suriyoru, a hilltop park whose pathetic claim to fame was that a minor medieval warlord started building a castle on the hill, but only got as far as the foundations before he was pulverized in one of those convoluted political betrayals that seem to drive ancient Japanese history. Every three or four steps, the boy glanced back nervously.

As he rounded a bend in the trail, he stole a final glance over his shoulder, and disappeared. Such caution could only mean two things, sex or drugs. Either way, I wanted some, so I followed him.

The trail fed into a brightly lit service road that wrapped around the murky man-made lake at the center of the park. An older man kept a lakeside vigil on a bench. I am sure he wanted casual passersby to think he was just drinking in the sliver of moon, but he was in fact a study in waiting. One man, and then a second passed him by. He watched cautiously, his gaze clinging to their backs as they disappeared on the shadowy trails that wound up the hill. Distracting his appetite with Marlboros, he gently pushed out the milky smoke and let it curl about his lips.

I hid my bicycle in some bushes, and followed the path of the men. As the lights of the service road faded behind me, I marveled at my own lunacy. Never before had I pursued unknown men into unknown woods in the dark, but already my erect cock bobbed before me in my sweats. It was my compass, directing me with its simple, one-eyed tunnel vision, negating my flight instincts and other sensible impulses. Perhaps my cock and I had come into a genetic memory of queer men, for without anyone telling me, I knew the rules: the darkness is our friend; speak little; trust smells; risk.

Halfway up the hill, a Roman orgy was nowhere to be seen. I broke off from the main trail to a tiny footpath which dead-ended beneath a cloister of branches, where a salaryman slouched on a bench. His tie was half undone and his legs were spread wide in a V of invitation. I began to turn back, embarrassed about breaking his solitude, but then I stopped.... He was just like me. I wanted sex. He wanted sex. The man by the lake and the nervous boy wanted sex, too. I did not know how to get what I wanted, but I figured that physical proximity might facilitate the process. I sat down next to him.

Time warps curiously during sexual predation. For five minutes or an hour, we sat and took turns looking at each other's profiles, growing bolder as time passed. Eventually we were both staring openly at each other-so rude in both our countries. He was perhaps forty, with wire-rimmed glasses. Under the guise of shifting himself, he inched his way across the bench toward me. It was a glacial process, but finally I could smell the whiskey on his breath and feel his sleeve against my thigh. I wanted to grab him or run, but I felt too shy to grab and too horny to run, so I waited, anxious to learn how a man takes a man.

The feel of his hand on my knee was a welcome break in the sexual tension. He kneaded my leg, softly at first but then more firmly, past the top of my thigh to my inner thigh. From there, he slid his hand onto my crotch. Cold sweat. His thumb and fingers pulsed open and closed like an anemone in shallows. He stood abruptly, pulled me up with him and pushed my sweats down to my knees. The night air on my legs and ass felt shameful. I tilted my head forward to kiss him, a ridiculous, movie-driven gesture. He turned his head. With one cold hand under my shirt on the small of my back, he pressed me against himself. With his other hand, he teased and pumped me into an orgasm that left me panting in his arms, my lips pressed greedily into his stubbled cheek.

A winter of raw apprenticeship passed and I entered a stage of connoisseurship. I walked the inky trails with the sureness of a blind man in his bedroom. I knew where knotty cedar roots reared up into walking trails to trip me. I knew where sycamore branches spread above and around me like gnarled, protecting fingers. I savored the sweet secret hush of nights in fog. I could spy on coupled men with the unassuming watchfulness of rocks.

IV

Until he moved in the darkness, I thought Atsushi was part of a maple trunk. He walked to me with the confidence of a man who enjoys being six foot two. He did not come to me to be physically engulfed, but met my breadth with his height. He did not wait to be swept along on the force of my foreign passion, but slipped my shirt above my head, and pinned my upraised arms to the tree. He unzipped himself with his free hand, like a rapist. His erection arched as sweetly as a dolphin breaching water. We grappled like wrestlers, yielding nothing to each other without resistance. He punished me, biting every place he kissed and kissing every place he bit. I asked him for his number.

On our first date, we met at a playground near Suriyoru. Atsushi brought me a firework. It was a wooden rod with a string hanging from the end. A little red box with a fuse hung from the string. He placed the rod in my hand and lit the fuse, which sputtered and then lit up. The red box spun furiously on the end of the string, trailing red and gold sparks and making a wonderful humming sound. The sparks died out and I breathed in the delicious sulfurous smell. Atsushi took the rod from my hand and held the smoking red box to my face. It had split open into a miniature birdcage with red strings for bars and a tiny paper bird in its interior.

I marveled at the birdcage and thanked him profusely. We drove across the Kofu Valley to the foot of the Minami Alps, where I asked him our destination. With his head, he gestured toward the mountains. As we wound our way up the pass, fewer and fewer houselights broke the darkness. Steering with his right hand, Atsushi fumbled with my zipper and worked his fingers into the flap of my boxers. He pulled me out and stopped the car mid-road. Slipping back my foreskin, he took a fingerful of precum and smeared it across his upper lip. He closed his eyes, and tilted his head back. The hazard lights blinked and blinked and blinked while he sat still and breathed.

V

In a month, my mouth and hands had completely learned Atsushi's body. Beyond that, I knew only his age (thirty-one) and a phone number that invariably connected me with a robotic female voice on his answering machine. Personal questions were clumsily deflected back to me with a nervous smile.

"What music do you like, Atsushi?"

"I don't like music. What music do you like, Jaime San?"

"Do you live with your family?"

"Don't you get lonely living alone in Japan, Jaime?"

I knew nothing of him, and was free to imagine everything. I conjured entire lives for Atsushi, and wrapped them about him like paper doll outfits. Atsushi was married with children. Atsushi was a bachelor, living with his parents and grandmother. Atsushi was a cop. Atsushi was cheating on his boyfriend.

When we kissed, I rubbed my rough goatee into his soft, pale cheek. Hard. I knew that this hurt him, yet as his cheek grew raw, he rubbed harder and harder, confused sobbing sounds erupting from his throat. Only a man could hurt him this way.

Atsushi's mind was a place unknown to me, but the rest of his body could keep no secrets, for even his most subtle muscular shifts rippled plainly beneath the skin. I marvel still at the long, protean slenderness of him. His body held everything: a boy's smoothness, a woman's curves, and a man's wiry strength. I saw that "we" existed only through sex. When I left him, only my hands and mouth mourned his absence.

VI

In a tiny bookstore in Kofu, I finally found gay Japanese porn. With all the discretion of the country teacher that I was, I placed it under a seven-dollar copy of *Time* magazine and took it to the counter. The divinely stoic checkout girl registered no emotion as she rung up and bagged my magazines. I bicycled home at full speed, tearing into the book bag before my apartment door had even closed behind me. To my horror, the centerfold's genitals were obscured by coarsely cut screening films. No matter; I masturbated several times, my hungry eyes liberating their cocks. I moved on to the editorial part of the magazine. There was an amazing installment of a serial comic. It appeared to be about a high school wrestler with a crush on his coach. The boy and the coach were hugging and looking ready for sex when the coach's girlfriend busted in on them. The coach left with the girl, and the boy was left crying beneath a cascade of falling cherry blossoms. Beautiful.

Nestled within the infuriatingly incomprehensible tangle of kanji personal ads, I saw an ad in English! *Tokyo Friends is a club for Japanese gay men and their foreign friends. Please come to our meeting on the last Sunday of the month and meet new friends. Bringing Friends!!* Two Sundays later, I was on the train to meet Tokyo Friends.

At Tokyo Friends, I was the only foreigner under the age of forty-five. The Japanese men in attendance were far more diverse in age, ranging from their early twenties to their late fifties. Tokyo Friends was a scene of awful disappointment. The Japanese men came expecting James Dean types and got old, rather lascivious men. I was equally disappointing to them, for though I was young, I wasn't really American. I wasn't white, let alone Aryan. The white queers also faced horrible disenchantment. Huddled together at their own table, they butted their balding heads against the limits of their privilege. These were Japanese, the proudest, richest queers in Asia, and unlike their needier counterparts in Thailand, the Philippines, or even Hong Kong, the Japanese were unimpressed by the foreigners' money or their white skin. Lunch was a particularly dreadful affair, with the Japanese quietly enduring and the foreigners breathlessly recounting how much easier dating was in Bangkok and Manila.

VII

In the ten years since I left Japan, I have radically revised my views of the sexual power of Asian men. Clubs, personal ads, and interactions at parties and in gay ghettos provide a bleak picture indeed. Gay Asian sexuality seems to me a gift that is wrapped up and proffered for the consumption of white gays and, to a lesser extent, blacks and Latinos. In one personal ad after another, the inexplicable gay Asian penchant for white men manifests itself with extraordinary consistency. Equally consistent is the lack of ads by Asians seeking Asians. The gay Asian couple is scarce enough to be nearly mythic in my mind.

One Asian man said sex with another Asian man was "like

incest." Another felt it was "bumping pussies." During a discussion with two smart Asian-American men, one of them asked me, "Is there a Latino term that's the equivalent of sticky rice?" There isn't. Gay Asian men created the term *sticky rice* because a gay Asian man desiring and pairing with another gay Asian man is noteworthy. In other racial groups, same-race attraction is such a given that there isn't even a set phrase for it.

VIII

In contrast to my many sexual encounters with Japanese men, my sexual experiences with gay Asian-American men have been limited. I get noticed by queer Asian-American men mostly when I stand between them and a white guy. I do not lament this, as I have no particular fetish for Asian men. My prolific sexual experiences with Japanese gays were happy accidents of geography. If I had been in Kenya, I would have pursued black men. In Mexico, I would have chased down my brothers, but I was in Japan, a rigidly ordered country where I somehow found sexual freedom and a richness of experiences that have left me envying no one.

Rainbow's End

Allen de Souza

Six, seven, eight. The church clock's familiar chimes echoed through the trees. Nine, ten. Luke counted them automatically, not bothering to open his eyes: eleven. Still an hour before he had to return home, pretending that he had been to Mass. If it weren't for the clock's warnings, he might have sat in the cemetery for hours, listening to the birds, bathing in the different flower scents. Even surrounded by dead people, it was miles better than the musty, decaying smells of church and those boring, never-ending prayers. Kneel sit stand, kneel sit stand. Amen. Church, as far as he was concerned, was the first place to find hypocrites and the last place to find God. Not that he was searching for God anymore, of course.

He pointed his face toward the sun, enjoying the warm redness, like moist tongues on his closed eyelids. A shadow fell across his face; a slap of perfume, the smell already heavy in his lungs. The bench boards creaked and pushed up against his buttocks as someone sat down.

He opened his eyes a fraction and glanced over. A man was wedged into the far corner of the bench, like a boxer between rounds; alert, almost predatory, but so confident in himself that he exuded waves of calm, even indifference. One arm draped over the back of the bench toward Luke, the other slid along the armrest; his legs were casually splayed. Luke's eyes played over the faded blue jeans-from the silver cowboy belt buckle (which seemed a little ridiculous in a grown man), to the bulge at the fly and down the arc of muscular thighs. The man, in turn, was intently watching Luke and had clearly noticed the direction and sweep of his glance. He smiled, "You looked so peaceful, quite angelic. I'm sorry to disturb you." Luke, slightly ashamed about where his eyes had been, looked away, but must have automatically, politely, returned the smile. The man threw back his head, pushed up his chest toward the sun; "Ahh, perfect," he sighed, as if he were reclining on a beach somewhere. "Beats church any day," and he shot a conspiratorial wink at Luke. Luke started. Was the man a truant officer from the church—and was there even such a thing—or a spy sent by his parents? "Relax," the man said, noticing Luke's reaction, "I'm skiving off too."

They began chatting aimlessly and easily, about the weather, the park; the man asked innocent questions about Luke's school, his friends, hobbies. Luke did relax, offering his own innocuous anecdotes and pleasantries.

"Do you like girls?" Luke had never been asked such a question, and certainly not that directly. He didn't know what to answer. He mumbled what he thought was a noncommittal yes. He didn't really know what it meant to like girls; he used to like being with them and playing their games, but since he had started going to a boys-only school he no longer knew any girls. The man laughed at his hesitation and asked jokingly, "You like boys then?" Luke felt his face flush and looked intently at the ground as if he had suddenly seen something that demanded his full attention. Now he knew what the man meant, and his face felt even hotter. Offhandedly, the man suggested a drive, promising to return Luke within the hour. Luke—who had never been warned against accepting lifts from strangers, and for whom such a warning would only have spurred his interest anyway—accepted readily.

The car, an open-top sports model-Luke doesn't remember what kind, just its long, sleek shape, and that it was bright red; or did that vision only come later?—sped through the small town and within minutes they were leaving shops and houses for open fields. The seats were so low and leaned right back; he felt he was reclining on a magic carpet which hovered mere inches off the ground. If he dangled his arm out the window he was sure his fingers would scrape the road.

The man placed his hand warmly on Luke's knee for a moment and lifted it up to brush his fingers against Luke's cheek. Luke grinned back at him. It was the greatest feeling speeding along the road, the wind rushing through his hair. And the man was so friendly.

They turned off the main road and into a narrow lane with grass growing along the middle. The hedgerows on either side were too high to see over, but in the rush of green there were sudden breaks, almost subliminal, through which Luke snatched glimpses of iron gates with fields and horses behind. The road began to climb and zigzag blindly. They would be rushing toward the end of the road, toward a hedge or a tree; Luke would press himself back into the seat, alternately wide-eyed or with eyes tightly shut until suddenly, moments before impact, the man would swing the wheel and the car would sheer off to the left or the right and a new stretch of road would appear. Though he knew that the road wouldn't suddenly end, Luke couldn't help feeling that they would drive off an edge or that they might turn a corner and crash into a car coming the other way. He gripped his seat, but the man sat loosely, relaxed, as if unaware of such possibilities, and the car continued its aggressive speed.

The man changed gears, and with a rattling cough as if it were winded the car slowed to a crawl. It turned onto a dusty track under a dark canopy of trees, and rumbled through the rustling, leafy tunnel; at the end, growing larger and brighter as they approached, were the curves of the horizon and the uninterrupted blue sky above. The trees abruptly ended as if sliced away by a giant ax. The man stopped the car and jumped out over the closed door. Luke followed, a little clumsily.

Before them, like the entrance to a fairy tale, was a vista of rolling hills speckled with cows and distant farmhouses leaking trails of lazily curling smoke. The sun was warm honey oozing down Luke's back. Like a small animal, he sniffed the air, cataloging each smell: dry, ticklish odor of hay bales, earthy cowpats, sharp tang of ripening apples.

The man ambled toward the shade of an oak, sprawled lazily onto the grass and beckoned to Luke. They chatted about things which Luke can no longer remember. At some point, without a break in their conversation, the man reached out as if it were the most natural thing in the world and cradled his fingers around Luke's balls as if weighing them. Luke didn't know what to do or what to expect; he felt apprehension but also the beginnings of a new, unknown excitement. The man's assurance and the size of his body promised something so different from the boys he pretend-wrestled.

The man jiggled his fingers gently and when Luke offered no

resistance, unzipped the fly and pulled out the little, already stiffening cock. He bent down and took the whole thing into his mouth, right up to the sparsely sprouting hairs at its base. He drew back and then down again, pushing the foreskin back with his lips and curling his tongue around the exposed head. He did it so smoothly, like a gourmet.

Whatever fears Luke might have had of danger-someone finding them, his face with *homo* slapped across it on the TV news, or even that this was really very strange—all these were swept away by the sensations gathering at his groin. He felt naughty, excited, faint—from pleasure, he thought.

The man stopped abruptly and unzipped his own jeans. "Here, do the same for me," he said, pulling down his white briefs. Luke gaped at the fleshy thing and wondered if it would fit into his mouth. It was fat and wrinkled. Ugly. The top was bald and shiny, and didn't have a skin covering like his own. Not something he would normally ever consider putting in his mouth, but now there was a strange compulsion to the prospect and the man had already shown him how much pleasure it gave.

He wet his lips and spread them over the blushing head. It was salty, bitter, sour, the tastes erupting from all over his mouth. Squishy and firm, like sucking liver. Or an eye. Faintly repulsed and at the same time thrilled, Luke copied what the man had done. He sucked down onto the thickening pillar of flesh, ascending and descending. Operating an elevator.

"Yeah. That's right. Do it. Oh yeah," the man kept repeating, the words running into each other, turning into long growls and moaning breaths. It wasn't long before Luke felt tremors in the man's body. He stopped, thinking they were surges of pain, and withdrew his mouth. The man let out a little moan of irritation. "Why did you stop?" he asked. As Luke, feeling suddenly embarrassed, searched for an answer, his attention was drawn back to the penis. He watched, fascinated, as it jerked a couple of times and slowly deflated, flopping over his hand. Something whitish seemed to be leaking out of the tip, but Luke thought it was just his own spit.

A frown, then a smile passed across the man's face as he watched Luke's mix of consternation and curiosity. "Here, let me show you," he said. He could have been a genial uncle patiently explaining a card trick. He licked his lips and pulled them inward over his teeth. Like a gummy old man, he again took Luke's cock in his mouth, a little more firmly this time, and with his cushioned teeth slid the foreskin up and down. The tingling ran down the shaft and began to vibrate somewhere behind Luke's balls. Sharp jabs of pain—but they felt good-gripped the base of his cock. His bladder felt full, its weight pressing down, a pump forcing the liquid. He squeezed his thighs, clenched all his muscles, but couldn't hold back the flood. The man's mouth moved faster, down up lick lick down. Luke squeezed again but it was no use, there was no stopping now. Abruptly, the man jerked his face away, coughing and spluttering. Luke watched a fountain of golden liquid arcing out, splashing hotly onto the two of them, even as the man scrambled out of the way. Luke, laughing, turned to direct the stream onto the grass. It felt delicious, though he wasn't sure exactly why. Was it merely the sudden release, the relaxing of his body, or was it something else? The strange, unexpected delight of drenching the man, and himself?

The man clearly didn't share his pleasure, though he seemed more bemused than annoyed. "You liked that, huh?" he said, still coughing, and staring, as if reassessing Luke. Luke smiled, and shrugged: *Wasn't that supposed to happen?* There were so many other questions in Luke's head, so many answers he wanted, but there weren't any words for them. The man, grumbling something about getting back, didn't seem quite so friendly anymore.

They dressed in silence, Luke's wet trousers already losing their heat and turning clammy. In the car, the man turned to Luke as if to speak, then seemed to change his mind and turned his attention back to the road. After long minutes of quiet with the words jumping around inside his head, Luke finally said, "So, er, you want to meet next week?" The man looked across, his mouth smiling but his eyes seeming far away, "You'd like that? Well, why don't I find you again? I've seen you at the cemetery lots of times." It was hard to tell if the man really meant it, but Luke left it at that. It had been fun, and he would like to do it again.

The man dropped Luke a block away from his house. Luke ran down the alleyway behind his street, clambered over his back fence, slipped open the front door, and ran upstairs unnoticed. Everyone was in the kitchen or in the dining room setting the table. Luke washed hastily, gargled with mouthwash, and changed into fresh clothes. Satisfied there were no lingering smells or other traces of his adventure, he went downstairs to join the family for Sunday brunch.

The fried egg white slurped off the fork, greasing his lips as it slithered into his mouth. He pinned it to the roof of his palate and licked to and fro along its underbelly, then pushed it unchewed to the back of his throat and felt it shimmy down. He speared a sausage and closed his lips over one end, punctured the skin with his teeth and felt the hot juices erupt and splash the inside of his cheeks. He bit through, tumbling the fleshy head onto his eager tongue, and slowly, slowly sucked it dry.

The image and memory—the taste, the touch, the smell—of the man's penis were not easily dispelled, and kept surging into Luke's mind during the following days. Even as, over time, the image lost its details and faded from immediate recall, perhaps insinuating itself into a deeper place, Luke began increasingly to stare at men's crotches, seeking revealing shadows or mysterious forms.

The swelling at his groin, he soon learned, was directly connected to the images in his head. Everywhere he went, men were walking around with their own large bulges, their hardness-the length, the breadth, the weight—clearly discernible through the folds or the tightness of their trousers. What were the images in their heads as they went through the motions of daily life? He imagined holographic projections beaming from the head of each man—jerking bodies with tentacling cocks—rioting in the air above the streets while the women around them calmly, unknowingly, continued their lives.

At about the same time, having read about the health benefits of urine—its regular consumption by yogis, the reabsorption of vitamin B and various mineral salts—Luke begins to drink his own. He has become quite discerning, a piss connoisseur, imitating adults at a wine tasting.

First thing in the morning, he locks himself in the bathroom, places an old Washington Monument souvenir glass in the basin and pisses in it. He picks up the glass, marveling that liquid that hot could come out of him. Holds it up to the light, nods sagely at its deep yellow, almost orange, color. Lifts the glass to his nose, sniffs appreciatively: hmm, a faint tinge of the licorice he had been chewing the night before. Touches the glass to his lips, sips daintily. It's a bit like the vegetable broth he has to drink when he's sick: salty and vaguely cabbage flavored. He sloshes it around in his mouth, gargles. Spits it out. Having stewed overnight in his bladder, it's too strong for his taste. He prefers the lighter, less vegetable flavor of his mid-morning, post-breakfast, fruit-juice urine-the bright lemon yellow, its fresh-from-the-body bouquet, its piquant, almost tart taste.

Later, when he discovers semen for the first time—though that is another story—he will become acutely embarrassed to recall his hillside baptism. Until then, he thinks pissing is the culmination of sex.

And God? God—or at least a little taste of heaven—continued to be sought in encounters at the cemetery. Ah, men.

Scents and Sensibility

Sonny Alberto Vajrabukka

Jo stretched as he emerged in a cloud of steam from the shower, trying to exorcise the day's stress from his muscles and joints. Unpacking and pricing CDs all morning long left him a little sore. He disliked doing inventory. At least when he was stocking the floor he could scam on any cuties that walked in. His branch had an extensive rap/hip hop section, and that was where most of the cuties headed. Jo would re alphabetize a section as many as eight times in one shift, lying in wait for some bebot to have trouble finding a CD. Jo smiled a lot and leaned in close whenever he was helping a customer. He'd always try to get a name off of them. It was a little funny to him how they all had the uniform: cargo pants or jeans, hiking boots, and puffy jackets in some shade of Skittles. Caps or headbands often finished off the look. They all even smelled the same, using either one of two colognes whose ads featured people that didn't look anything like the people who actually wore them. Jo always found himself grinning through the day, silently giggling at them and at himself. Jo had much of the same gear in his own overstuffed dresser, piled on top of old midterms and his dog-eared, raggedy old copies of *Loose Woman*, *Pedagogy of the Oppressed*, and *Epistemology of the Closet*.

As he patted the lush towel over his body, Jo sighed. He often got contemplative like this after his showers, standing naked in front of the mirror. A large citrus-scented candle burned on the countertop. He recalled scenes of puffy jackets, socks, T-shirts, sandos, jeans, and boxer shorts strewn along the hardwood floors from front door to bathroom door. Jo ran his right hand over his wet fuzzy head. It would soon be time to shave it again. He wrapped the towel around his waist and leaned toward the purple tulip that sat in a glass tumbler next to the sink. As he felt the silky petals on his nose, he looked into his own eyes, listened to the rise and fall of his breath for a few moments, and then opened the bathroom door.

Jo threw the damp towel onto the bed and pressed a button on the boombox. Born Jamericans began sending their love as he glided over to the dresser. He was thankful it was a warmer night than usual. Grabbing the moisturizer, Jo squeezed a quarter sized portion into his hand and slowly rubbed his palms together, allowing the aroma to suffuse the room. He put his hands to his face and inhaled deeply. A smile crept across his lips. The scent was familiar, pleasing. Arousing.

On his dresser Jo had a large Virgen Maria votive candle, a tube of body lotion, and a bottle of lube. He would silently snicker at these little daily reminders of the great loves of his life. These were not birthday gifts or anniversary presents. These items did not come with dinner or a card. They mysteriously appeared on his dresser at some point during the relationship, and managed to stay, even after the other mementos were either returned or burned. There were no painful memories here anymore, only these three things and Jo's sense of humor. Bitterness was as alien to Jo as white dick.

Jo squeezed a line of Acqua di Gio across his palm, noting the shiny creaminess and how it curled into a pointed tip. Left over right, he spread it over his fingers, then over the knuckles and the backs of his hands. He chuckled because the brand name echoed the Vietnamese word for egg rolls (cha-gio).

He rubbed it into his shoulders, kneading the curves carved by laps in the pool.

The lotion grew milky with each pass, fading into the golden brown flesh. His fingers squeezed firmly, muscles rolling under his palms as he worked his way up near his neck and then down the length of his arms. Jo watched himself in the mirror, his skin shiny and reddish in the candlelight, and was pleased with the fine lil' island person that he was.

A second line, and in one stroke he smeared it across his chest. His fingers traced the outer edges, lingering a moment to circle his nipples, before fanning out over the center and down his stomach. He watched his skin glow brighter as it drank the moisture, and noticed how the smooth lines and velvety surfaces resembled the washed-out back roads in his parents' homeland after a monsoon. The fragrant, sweet scent hung thick in the still apartment air, and he could almost see it rising off his cooling naked torso. Jo smelled this way after sex with the most recent ex. He liked coming home with this man's, his man's, scent seared into his skin after hours of slippery, steamy, fluid-filled fun. If it was a weekend he would not shower, spending the day half naked sniffing his shoulders, arms, and hands, until Sunday evening, when he finally had to jack off.

Line number three, and he rubbed the fluid onto his upper legs, his hands flat against the still damp flesh, spreading the slick, aromatic substance over his legs and hips, fingers curving to hug the contours closely when he reached his ass and the small of his back. Jo closed his eyes. His fingers became his lover's fingers gripping those cheeks firmly, one finger nestled in between, as they sandwiched their erections between two sweaty bodies sliding over each other. Those were the fingers that also spread those same cheeks wide so that big brown lips could kiss Jo's little brown lips. How many times afternoon class and morning mass were forgotten because of this, Jo could not recall.

Jo opened his eyes and saw the reflection of his hard-on looking back up at him. It was darker than the rest of him, like the color of his nipples, but softer to the touch, like his lips. He stepped closer to the mirror. All his lovers had commented on how it leaned slightly to the right, and how smooth and shiny the head was. He had not been this fascinated with looking at his dick since adolescence, and could not quite get why more than a few of his lovers and some of his tricks would pause in the middle of sex to just look at it like it was some detailed impressionist painting. It was "cute," some of them had said. Many mornings he even used to wake up with his shorts around his knees and the ex, the fragrant one, propped up between his legs talking to his pee pee.

Jo crossed the candlelit studio, the floors creaking underfoot. He spread the towel out on the bed. He lay himself on the edge, legs dangling over the side. In the mirror, he looked to himself like a long shadow across the white down comforter. He squeezed out line number four and rubbed his palms together.

His body tensed as he wrapped his cold, moist right hand around his erection. He held it there a couple moments, listening to himself breathe and savoring the contrast of sensations. His left hand glided over his stomach, flattening the curves of his chest as it pressed its way over his nipples. He put his left hand to his face and inhaled deeply. Jo's toes curled and his lips slowly curved up into another smile as his right hand began moving. In his mind, beanie caps and plastic glasses with yellow-tinted lenses began falling onto hardwood floors.

Bite

Justin Chin

Cumon fuck me daddy fuck me good daddy fuck me daddy fuck your boy daddy fuck your boy real good daddy fuck me good daddy fuck me fuck me daddy yeah daddy fuck your boy real good daddy fuck me hard daddy fuck me daddy fuck me hard fuckme daddyfuck real good&hard daddyfuck daddy-fuckme gooddaddy fuckmefuck medaddyfuckme daddy-fuckmedaddy yeahfuckmefuckmefuckme.

((I'm just one dumpy chink, you want to fuck me? got nothin but one big wet tight butthole for you to poke your big dick in. Stick it right in all the way in 'cos that's what it's good for.))

Rugs swears this story is true & then I kind of believe him 'cos I know the guy too & then I asked some buddies who knows him too & they all said they *heard* & then I know it's probably true too 'cos too many people *heard*. Rugs said it was that one trick one fat dude like Move really likes them so that was cool 'cos we all got our types we like like me like them real big & tough & got some mean badass streak in them Rug likes them real skinny like somekind of stickmen as if one squeeze & they crack in two but Move gets this one fatass dude who wants him real bad & the rest everybody seems to know.

{{I love sniffing Chinese ass because they're always so smelly. You got one smelly ass chink boy? you got one stinkin wet ass for daddy brownboy? motherfuckin' chink boy you fart loud huh?

you like to smell daddy's farts? daddy wants to smell your farts boy. How do you fart chink-boy huh? make that sound for daddy, yeah, that's it little stinky-chink, you can do better, what's that pst-pst little fucking sound, pathethic, chink boy you can do better.}}

Schitt cumon. You know my scene & this ain't it ain't it at all godamm schitt. Cumon, you gotta hit me real good yeah with the back of your hand godammit, what you think I'm your fucking bigbone puffy poodle or what, shithead. Okay, now hang on wait let me sit on dick first yeah that's it now you do it real good man, yeah lemme have it.

[& then he really starts getting into it & all & he's really whopping me real good but it doesn't hurt one bit 'cos he don't know how to really do it good, like my man can. This one's just playing small-bit & he knows not to mark me 'cos then he can't fall in *lurve* with me too late for that now big boy 'cos someone's got to cum got to go home tonight for some real good fucking.]

{{You wanna suck daddy's dick, you wanna suck daddy dick while daddy's sitting takin a shit? better tell me now: better decide now 'cos once I start shittin & it's real stinky, you're not going to stop sucking on my fat daddy dick, so tell me now, say sir boy tell me now if you like the smell of my ass, boy.}}

This is it man. Move meets this one dude & they go to his place & Move will try anything a few times 'cos he's some dumb schitt that thinks it's all okay & then this guy starts real good & nice like he's a loverman-supreme. kissy kissy huggy huggy &

that Move's one dumb schitt & he falls for that kind of stuff & you know to never fall for that schitt 'cos it doesn't mean anything but this Move falls & he gets real hot which is another no-no 'cos they know when you get hot. Myself I rather suck dick or lick butt than play that kissy schitt Move got into 'cos that's where the trouble starts & yeah right as schitt this guy really gets into it & everybody gets fucking hard & then there's the sucking & the fingering & the titwork & all of that usual schitt & then the dude proposes & says *it won't hurt a bit & it's really hot & it's like nothing* Move says he's not sure but then he's too hot to say no really properly & then the chopstick is out & into his dickhead & all the way down his shaft.

((I jus' one funny-looking chink, but if I tell you the real truth, you still wanna fuck me? you prob'ly jus' spit on my ass and leave. cum sum'where else.))

<- - - *Where are you calling from? What do you get into? I'm into fascist violence man. I want to kick someone in. Stomp on someone's face. Yeah, that's cool buddy. If you get it right, you can pop an eyeball like bubblewrap. Haha. Ever done that? I don't ever wash my jeans 'cos I like the bloodstains. What do you look like? Ever rape someone's brown shitass after you kick the shit out of him? Cool man. Fuck that ass until it's bleeding like his face. Yeah buddy. Can I call you. Do you like to party. Yeah I wanna cum with you....*>

{{Yeah, you like me to plug your butt with my toys? See this one? It's too fucking big for you, it'll just tear your sweet little ass & then I can't play with you 'cos you'll just scream & say no-no-

no, you're just one pantypussyass, you know. You sure you can take it? I don't want to hear no complaints now. See this hole here in the head? Fake piss-slit. I shove it up your ass then I fuck in the back here & then I cum into it & then it shoots out, well drips out, here into your ass, yeah, you think that's hot? Then I want to scrape my cum out of your ass and make you eat it.}}

This one guy's got this weirdass thing going. Zee this real cute guy even I love the schitt right out of him has this real big thing for cum, loves drinking it & splashing it all over his body but that's cool 'cos myself I like that kind of thing, yeah nothing like a real good load to turn my spine you know, but this guy's got a bottle he swiped from some doctor friend (ha!) & he keeps cum in it & he gets his tricks & friends & himself to cum into it & fills it up then he drinks it all, I know 'cos I cumed into it couple of times & then later I watched the guy drink it all chug it all down & this is like it's a week old & the bottom is all clear & things really stick & clump & looks like spit with bubbles & all, I tell him Keep the fucking thing in the fridge man! but he says it's like cheese or wine, gotta age it right. Hell, whatever it takes to get you off, right?

Now Move is all hot & all & the guy really cums a load that Zee would've killed for & Move starts to dribble out of the edges of the stick in his dick & the guy rips the stick right out of his dick & Move screams like mad & dig this: the bamboo chopstick splinters into his dick & Move cries like mad for days & everytime he gets a hard-on it tears the shit right out of his dick and balls & he can't move & then the guy gets scared &

runs off & Move is so fucked but then why did he have to get hot for, damn stupid schittass. And he should've used a lacquered chopstick instead, that stupid schitt.

{{Kiss daddy's nuts boy yeah kiss them real good kiss daddy's juicebag kiss it like you really wanna drink daddy's juice boy.}}

((Fuck me fuck me let me feel you daddy let me feel your cock daddy let me feel your dick all the way up me daddy take it off daddy let me feel you daddy let me feel you cum up my ass.))

I tell this story to my man all the way up to the bit where Move gets the operation & now his dick looks like some deformed baby's hand & my man's balls all tighten & move up into his crotch real cute but then we understand each other real good & I pull them out with my tongue just like he likes & then the cocks gets good & hard & there's a good sweat going & I know he knows how to hurt me like I like it.

Liberty

John Tunui

My adopted parents treated me to a vacation in New York. We had been friends for three years, and one day at my Fourth of July party, I introduced them, in front of all my gay friends, as "my new adopted parents, whether they like it or not."

"Honey, you look just like your mother," one of my "sisters" said. Both my adopted parents are white.

It was my first time in New York, a most magical city, and I absolutely fell in love with it. I'd bought myself a poster of the Statue of Liberty and was taking a break from sightseeing in Washington Square when I spied a guy looking me up and down. I had seen him on the subway, and also on Christopher Street, and now he was sitting on the bench across from me. Wow, I thought, I could get to appreciate this fair city even more.

The guy was bold, and his confidence caught me off balance. As for myself, I couldn't believe I was suddenly overcome with shyness and starting to blush. He noticed, came up to me and asked if I needed directions or something. Damn, I thought: he stole my line. The park was crowded and I wanted to try to make it look as if the guy was really giving me directions, so I unfolded a map. He pointed to it and said, "My place is not far from here."

He spoke with an accent. At first I couldn't place it. His eyes, deep blue, bored through me: I could not believe his speed. I thought I was quick, being a former Polk Street hustler, but this guy had me beat, and he wasn't charging. He introduced himself as Gaël, from Paris, and said he'd been living in New York for a year.

We wandered to a nearby café to get better acquainted, and he said he thought I'd been following him, and I said I thought he'd been following me, and one thing led to another, and finally he led me to his apartment-this absolutely gorgeous twenty-two-year-old French boy, with shoulder-length blonde hair, electric eyes, and a killer smile, and it seemed he was not a whore like me. (There's only one thing worse than sleeping with a cheap john, and that's sleeping with a fellow whore.) Anyway, Gaël's interest surprised me. I had been so busy cruising everyone in New York that I hadn't noticed someone had noticed me.

He was a student in English, living the poor-student life, and his small studio didn't have much furniture. His bed was just a mattress tossed on the hardwood floor.

We hit that bed, kissing quickly and passionately, undressing each other with practiced speed. He had a lean, smooth body and an uncircumcised penis. I assumed the bottom position while Gaël donned a condom and stroked on some lube.

"Take it easy, honey, I haven't had it in a while," I whispered through the curtain of his blonde hair dangling in my face. My legs were already wrapped around his neck.

"How long has it been?" he asked in his sexy and somewhat formal French accent.

"Oh, not since San Francisco," I replied.

"San Francisco is not as far as Paris."

"Oh, yeah? New Zealand is as far as one can get," I said. "Aaahhh, take it slow, once you get it in, keep it there for a while, okay? Please?"

Gaël silenced me by kissing me hard on the mouth while he penetrated me.

"You have many sheep in New Zealand, no?"

"Oh, too many, too many sheep," I moaned.

"New Zealand sheep like to get it up the ass, no?"

"I don't know, aaahhh, slowly, honey, slowly."

"This sheep is tight, no?"

"Just shut up and do me, honey."

"You sing me a New Zealand song while I make love to you, please."

"What? I don't know any New Zealand song. Just shove that thing into me."

"Please?"

"Okay, but I have to warn you I'm not a good singer. Bah bah black sheep...owww, no no, take it easy, have you any wool ahhh, no, no, please, no, ohhh yes yes yes sir, yes sir, three bags full give me three bags full sir, please sir, give it to me, one for the master, one for the dame and one for the little girl who lives down the lane, honey."

"You are a very bad sheep, no?"

"Bah, bah, yes sir."

"The master will have to punish the black sheep, no?"

"Bah, bah, yes sir, I've been a bad black sheep."

"Master must fuck black sheep up the ass, no?"

"Bah, bah, yes sir."

Our sweaty bodies climaxed simultaneously; I returned from cleaning up in the bathroom to find Gaël's beautiful lanky body at rest, a Gauloise jutting from his mouth at a jaunty angle. It was like a French film. I knelt to kiss him, and I was in awe that this sweet and beautiful angelic being had just fucked me like a beast.

I unrolled my poster of the Statue of Liberty and held it in front of me. I turned to face Gaël: "Liberty," I proclaimed.

"Liberté," he answered, with another cute smile.

"Liberty is a white French bitch standing in the water."

"Oh, you are from San Francisco and you are crazy," he said, and pushed his lovely white body off the bed and walked into the bathroom for a shower. I stuck the poster to the wall with a thumbtack from his cluttered study desk, then dropped back onto the bed with the TV remote, channel-surfing to the news. The headline was "Trouble in Paradise," about the Tahitian people protesting the French government's decision to test another series of nuclear bombs in the South Pacific. The footage showed native people attacking French functionaries in Tahiti.

I heard Gaël whistling in the shower, while on TV I watched police arrest a number of the protesters, one of them my Uncle Oscar, who was handcuffed and hurled into a police car. I was horrified. My uncle's face was pained, his kind and gentle eyes were now dark and sad and angry, a window into his anguish and suffering. Back in the bathroom Gaël was still showering.

As the images flickered, I wondered what would happen to Uncle Oscar and the rest of my people being arrested. I recalled how the French government had annihilated the native Kanaks of New Caledonia, its other South Pacific colony, some decades ago, and I remembered the dark cloud that showered dust on Aitutaki when I was just a kid, and I recalled the native Tahitians who came to New Zealand frantic for cancer treatment, cancer the French denied had anything to do with their bomb tests.

And I remembered more recent history, the attack on the *Rainbow Warrior* Greenpeace vessel in Auckland, New Zealand by the French secret services, killing or injuring the defenseless crew. The newscast showed file footage of a bomb exploding. A tall, white figure rose from the water. I gazed at the tall white figure of Liberty on the wall, looked back at the figure on the TV screen. "That white French bitch in the water," I whispered to myself.

Gaël turned off the shower, and I turned off the TV as he stepped into the studio, drying himself with a towel.

"Baby, please get me some wine from the refrigerator," he asked as he dried his body, his hair falling over his face as he bent to dry his toes, before raising one leg and toweling his testicles.

"Are you okay, my baby?"

"Yeah, yeah, I'm fine." I opened the fridge, brought out a bottle of wine, poured him a glass.

"Pour yourself one."

"No, thanks. I don't drink this," I said. He sipped his wine, smiled that sassy French smile, reached out with his hands and pulled our bodies back together. We kissed, quickly.

"Baby." He grinned. "You're not smiling." He grinned again, a sweet and innocent and beautiful smile, the sort that is so rare.

"Oh," I said, "I'm just letting you soak in, that's all. You were wonderful, and you're still wonderful."

I welcomed his comforting kiss, took his wineglass away, laid him down on the bed. We made love again, but this time I wore the condom and he wheeled and squealed while I penetrated him. He moaned and wept and tried to push me away. He swore in French and struggled to escape me, but I was too big and too strong and too upset about what was happening in Tahiti, and soon I ejaculated inside his white butt and he ejaculated into my hands. I rolled off his beautiful body and he went back to the bathroom.

"Baby, that hurt me real bad," he said when he came back, and then he beamed another of his sexy smiles. "But I liked it."

He walked over to the kitchenette, poured more wine and stood in front of the TV, next to the poster of the Statue of Liberty, the wet cotton towel draped over his shoulder, a cigarette suddenly lit in his raised right hand, the glass of wine at his side.

Liberty had never looked sexier.

And then he said to me: "That's why I prefer making love to a black man. You are best when you are angry."

A Hand in the Dark

Chen Lin

When you walk in, people notice you: the fresh-faced hunk with an ass that puts the moon to shame. You know people watch you when you pass by, and the way you stop in the middle of the bar, looking left, looking right, while all the eyes are looking you up and down, the tension is enough to make the music skip. Whose gaze will intersect yours and arouse your interest? It won't be mine, and I don't mind.

In a way we're alike, you and I. People watch when I enter a room too. Their eyes dilate the same way, scanning me from face to feet. Only the fascination is different. I'm not tall or proportionate like you, but I know my own body and how to exhibit my attributes. For one thing, I have a handsome face, rugged and tan, made all the more attractive with a clean crew cut, trimmed beard, and dark, deep-set eyes. I have big hands for someone my size-thick, man-sized hands, and they look even better with the black leather cuffs around my wrists. I work out, eat healthy. My frame and musculature is that of a thirty-year-old, only condensed—a more compact version of the type of men you come to find.

Every time I see you in here I suppress a smirk. No, it's not to out-butch the crowd in this bar-that wouldn't be possible. And it's not about copping an attitude. There's enough strut and stance out in the pretty-boy bars, no need to bring it in here. It is, though, about pride and conquest, about someone like me being with someone like you. I'm a midget only by definition, still the thought might make you squeamish, the image in your mind grotesque. But there are freaks around who look every bit as normal as you do, maybe even better looking, who occasionally call me up for a fuck. You probably can't fathom that, so I won't disturb the depths of your imagination. Not in this light.

The first night you came in, my friend saw how you stared down at me, the look of fascination and fright broken only when you turned away. "Shit," Roy said, just low enough for me to hear. "Boy needs a lesson in manners, don't you think, Mack?"

"The view makes up for it," I answered, appreciating your ass in jeans. Not that I wouldn't have leg-tackled you to the ground if you had pissed me off.

Some of the pretty boys who come here looking for action try to pal up to me, thinking I could use the company while they wait for someone do-able. You, on the other hand, are more businesslike: you walk in, look around, maybe buy a beer, talk to the guy you're cruising, and take off. No matter how many times we've seen each other, at least you don't play at being friends. I'm not one to be flattered or humored when bored queens, no matter how cute, saunter up and say, "I've seen you in movies, right? Willow and Wizard of Oz references don't endear them to me.

Sometimes a curious customer will chat with me, slowly steering the conversation toward what they really want to know. Wearing a custom-made bar vest and leather pants isn't nearly enough, nowadays, to communicate your proclivities. My red hanky, though, gives it away. Some guys ask blunt questions, getting off on hearing a midget talk about handballing. And I answer them. In detail. And if they really get into it, I offer to show them. More than once I've found playmates this way.

The other place I go to is just a block from here. They know me there too. It's the only sex club that doesn't turn me away with some lame excuse, like they're holding a private party that night or they're out of membership forms. Fuck, if looks are so important in a sex club, why turn out all the lights?

The Pen is a nothing-barred kind of place, with a tub, a sling, and a dentist's chair. Almost all the walls have glory holes, and there's just enough light to watch the action by, but not so much as to make anyone self-conscious. Still, it was overwhelming my first time. The only thing I could do was watch from the shadows. Now I walk in like it's my living room, bedroom, and bathroom all in one.

You like it there too, I found out.

I must admit I was surprised when I saw you at The Pen. First my bar and now this. But then it seemed perfectly normal to me, seeing some guy rubbing your face into his hairy armpit. The two of you were in the mirrored room with porno flickering on a monitor in the corner. The televised light washed your bodies a steely blue. The skinhead guy had one hand behind his head and the other in your hair, grinding your nose and mouth in his armpit. You were holding on to him for balance and struggling against him at the same time, your face smeared with your own drool and his sweat.

It was gorgeous.

For a week I imagined you wrist-bound and naked, crouched down to lick out my hollowed pits like they were a pair of food dishes, your face slick and glistening beatifically as I jacked off all over your chest. Some say you can tell a man's cocksize by his feet. On me it's the hands. On you, of course, everything is indicative: big lips, big nipples, big round ass.

And then I saw you again at The Pen, this time silhouetted in the entrance of the narrow hallway where I was taking a breather. You stepped into the dark, guiding yourself along the walls with your hands. I stood up on the bench to make way as you stumbled through, past the grappling bodies standing and leaning and kneeling in your way.

I sensed your approach by the sound of your boots and when your hand struck the deadend I heard a resolution. You turned and I reached out, grabbing a double-handful of your pecs, and pressing you up against the wall in front of me. I lifted your arms and began eating out your keen pits, giving as good as you gave to the toned skinhead in the mirrored room. I licked and sucked and gnawed with my maw until you were gasping and bucking, but you kept your hands over your head, needing more. You weren't going anywhere. I had your attention.

I tongued your feathered pits and worked your eraser nub nipples with my fingers. I knew they were raw when you shuddered and shrank from my hands so I leaned down and nursed them gently in my mouth, making you sigh, your breathing heavy and deep. I reached for your crotch. Your package strained against the fly's brass buttons. Briefly, I felt your hands on mine as you grasped the top of your fly and yanked it open. The well-worn denim fell easily to your feet. No underwear. With my hands on your narrow hips I climbed down, standing steel-toe to steel-toe, and began sucking on your thick, veiny cock. Soon you were face-fucking me, your balls jouncing on my chin, the muscles in my jaw and neck aching from the exertion. You wanted to come, I could tell, but I eased off to nibble around your nuts, trailing my tongue along the inside of your thighs, brushing my five o'clock shadow everywhere my mouth had been. I reached between your legs and massaged your ass, gently pulling you to one side. Awkwardly, you shuffled around, and then I had you where I wanted you.

With my face in your crack, you couldn't have cared less what my hands were doing. The more I licked and probed your hole and bit your asscheeks, the more you relaxed. I struggled to pull on a latex glove and slipped a bottle of lube from my pocket. You shifted back, bending over little by little, your spine arched like a cat stretching. I ducked under and guided you to the bench I'd stood on. You sat down and slouched against the wall, your legs open to me. I sucked your cock down slowly and smeared some warm lube on your pucker, finger-fucking you to the rhythm of my mouth.

You moaned and raised your knees higher to accommodate a second digit. Your ass-ring gripped and released my slick fingers like a mouth sucking cock. You slipped down lower, your hips sliding off the bench. Lower still, and you planted your feet against the opposite wall. You rocked along, bearing down on my hand, becoming more urgent. Three fingers. Any lower and you'd fall to the floor. Not satisfied with three, I kept my fingers up your ass, like a handle, and lifted your leg over my head, pivoting you to lie lengthwise on the bench, your back supported securely on the smooth-worn wood. You were so abandoned; your ass barely clenched when I moved you so suddenly. I poured some more lube in my hand half up inside you and massaged it into your stretched bunghole. You heaved, low *ahs* vibrating through your body and up my arm. Four fingers.

By the time my hand was completely inside, my man-sized fist pushing and twisting in your gut, you were making deep-chested *uuuhs* that shook the bench. You huffed and breathed with your whole body. Through this and the vibrations of your voice I felt a beating, your pulse surrounding my hand like I had thrust my fist into your heart. And it was real. Flesh and blood real. Not the wrist-bound slave pleasing me with his eager tongue, this was you taking pleasure from my hand, pleasure so profound it didn't matter what I looked like.

A crowd had gathered. In the narrow deadend the sound of guys jerking off enveloped us. Someone was standing over you, pinching your nipples; another had your soft dick in his mouth. A splash of cum wetted my shoulder, the slow warmth trickling down my arm. Then a commotion. Someone was climbing his way through the crowd, in or out I couldn't tell. Bodies jostled, a few low curses, and then there was a shove and I was on the ground. Disoriented, I was trapped in a tangle of tall boots and legs, a stampede of men aroused by your lowing. After a while, the movement settled and I picked myself up off the filthy floor. There was no use trying to find you, the men had already closed in, drawn to the one so completely abandoned in the dark that he accepted anyone and anything.

That night I left knowing you would remember this experience. Every time I've seen you since, I imagine you can sometimes feel the phantom of my fist inside you. But the face you turn to me is always the same, one of detached recognition. In your mind I'm just the leather-clad midget who hangs out at the bar you cruise, someone you could never imagine sexually, much less with you.

Asia/Pacific Overtures

Ferd Eggan

Last night I fucked a guy from Vietnam.

He came here in 1975, at the age of fifteen. Fucking, I remembered the work against the war, the criminals, the secret bombing and how thrilling it was to see the Vietcong men holding hands thinking that a people's war of liberation would rebuild a country ten times more beautiful with Uncle Ho and names like Perfume River, and here was Dong, who experienced the whole thing as suffering and closed possibilities.

Was I wrong?

Was my whole past pursuit of misrule, chaos, and error?

I couldn't be a rice queen; anyway, it's racist to be so specialized. L.A. is full of white guys who only do Asians, or only do Latinos, or only do Blacks.

But maybe I could: there is something particularly beautiful, the eyes, the skin, the cheekbones, the straight black hair, the maleness embodied so differently that their drag queens are unrecognizable to us. Wylie Wong back in 1969 dressing like the Peking Opera, exquisite. It takes a feudal history to develop sumptuousness, beauty beyond use and refinement. That's why the Japanese are the only Pacific Islanders to cultivate refinement (maybe some Indonesian islands—but that would be the history of religious conquest). Japanese men are butch like some other island cultures. They must have avidly lapped up all of China's arts, but with disdain, cutting them to the bone and stripping beauty to simplicity and controlled accident, a savagery visible now only in men's language. Do the Japanese fags speak men's or women's language? I understand they think we smell bad, are too big, too hairy, too clumsy.

Well, no matter, we occupied them. We gave them pop culture. No wonder Mishima posed first as St. Sebastian and then as an ultranationalist savior of the Emperor: only a disemboweling was hard-on enough to penetrate the Americanized asshole of that ultracosmopolitan culture that reaches its climax in the gigapet. He was butch, I could imagine him fucking me, sweat pouring off those perfect, slightly hairy muscles, his eyes stark and staring like the demons of the old prints. I could see myself exquisitely bound (the artfulness of wrapping three eggs), shaved by the edge of an eighteenth-century sword, my muscles gripped in his strong hands.

But the one that fucked me the best was a Chinese man who lived by the Cow Palace—tall, wiry, smooth, with a dick that was way big for me back in the days when I was first getting fucked. Centuries of tradition left him no need to be butch, just a man who knew how to fuck. And then he gave me beautiful porcelains.

White guys differ over these preferences: refined or savage. The rice queens almost always think they are butch and their Asian paramours are femme. There's a beauty to that, little fluttering butterflies, inscrutable erotic skills; is it surrender to be a top, to be a provider of pleasure? But I've always wanted the yellow Asian bodybuilders, or PI guys whose bodies are ripped and shredded so that muscles stand erect under perfect brown skin. I don't like the chunky ones, but I loved the taut nakedness of my for-real, genuine Hawaiian surfer, hanging ten, thighs that gripped and grappled as we sucked and fucked in absurdly steamy, sweaty heat. Our bodies slid over each other like slugs, leaving sexy trails of moisture in every crevice, locked in each other's dripping armpits, slipping in and out of every hole, the Pacific championship of wrestlemania, big sets of waves, man.

The savage, the primitive. In the little huts in Vietnam, how many? How our GIs must have cum, over and over, cum spilling out of the Mekong Delta. In Thailand, a whole sex industry created by GI cum, beautiful boys receptacles for R&R dollars sent home to the highlands. My first boyfriend, Melvin, was a Black GI in Thailand in 1966, discovering himself and his beauty surrounded by admiring Thai boys. I know how he fucked, gently entering, taking his time until my pleasure demanded his urgency; how he must have fucked on vacations from the War, where he had to pretend he was unafraid. And then a holiday in Cambodia might have meant something more than skeletons. The secret bombing and the secret fucking are no more, just AIDS is left. Many of you who read this are here because of the bombing and the fucking. What have we done? Are you happy being Orientals, being Others?

And the ultimate, the last waste dump was always the Philippines. Sewers full of toxic American cum since 1898, using, finally losing the ninety-nine-year lease. We liked the little brown ones, we led them, we bled them, they sucked us dry. I wasn't there, I'll have you know. The advances were made by the soldiers, I stayed at home, protesting, but objectifying the fierce little partisans, primitive but savvy in their hatred.

But then I got my own "Flip," also a partisan, beautiful, perfect. I didn't, I still don't know what it meant to love outside the barriers, the national frontiers, and then suddenly it mattered a great deal because I did love, clumsily, frightened, eager to escape. You were beautiful; you still are. I swallowed, you swallowed, we opened. The dances always show off the allure of the primitive, the savage, all through the islands, the Hawaiians, the Fijians, the Samoans, the Papuans, the Filipinos: thrusting, showing off their manhood. They the raw; we the cooked. Brown and yellow, black-take my inauthentic white life and spear it onto yours. Now, as I grow older and need more titillation, I can imagine the smooth skin looming over me, the beautiful muscles sweating, dripping down on me as I offer my ass like all the shores washed by the Pacific.

Scherzo for Cunanan

Jason Guillermo Luz

I. Mostro: My Brother the Killer

There's nothing like a road trip to finally bring you to the breakdown that's been lurking on the horizon—lots of bland vistas and wide open road to pore and cry over. I thought you were over him, a friend told me, and I said, I guess I wasn't over getting over him.

The Great Salt Flats: Guess I'm in Utah now—Mormon country, the promised land out west. Nothing but salt and even more salt till kingdom come. In the blue light of dusk, the plains of salt glow like endless fields of dirty snow, but it must be eighty degrees.

Flipping through the radio stations, there's nothing but bad country western and Christian broadcasts. So I've resorted to listening to AM talk radio, but they keep repeating the same story. They think they've found the body of Andrew Cunanan, America's most wanted, the homicidal hustler who terrorized an entire country and put fear back in the hearts of gay men everywhere who had fallen back into their same old cruising habits.

Police in Miami have found what they believe to be the body of suspected serial killer Andrew Cunanan in a houseboat just miles away from the Versace estate. They think it was a suicide, gun through the mouth.

So I'm thinking if Andrew Cunanan hadn't gone and given head to his .40 caliber, I would've made it my mission to hunt him down, just so I could have a heart-to-heart with him.

It doesn't take much, he'd tell me, *civility is such a tenuous thing. It takes far less than you'd imagine to short out that tiny fuse in our psyches, the fuse that keeps us all plugging away in our happy little shells. That tiny little fuse that's the only thing keeping us from suddenly taking off cross-country, leaving a trail of dead bodies and outraged Americans.*

My poor misled mestizo brother, I would've said, appealing to his darker half, the half I could claim as kin, so a white boy went and broke your heart? It's hard isn't it—a white man's world and even more so when you're a faggot.

And he would've broken down right there across from me in the booth at some Podunk truck stop diner in Indiana or Ohio, running his hand anxiously over the bristle of his six-day stubble, his other hand trembling, sending cigarette ash into his lukewarm coffee.

He'd stare pensively out the window at the unbroken gray haze of the Indiana or Ohio skyline, the muscles of his jaw wriggling beneath the taut skin of his gaunt face. And without as much as an initial intake of breath or a contemplative sigh, he would rattle off his mini-saga of anger and alienation, spewing anecdotes and storylines like he was offering notes for a TV movie: the formative years in San Diego; too brown to be white, his shady businessman of a father gone back to the Philippine wilds; too white to be brown, his sainted derelict of a mother; the duplicitous and disjunctive life of the mixed-race child; the fiery shame of the sodomite.

He'd tell me stories of the rich seaside real estate moguls, the software engineers, investment bankers, and five-star restaurateurs, the Fortune 500 closet cases who wanted it all—trophy wives, rosy-cheeked, downy-haired children, tennis courts, hot teenage cock, virgin boy-pussy hymens intact and puckered small as babies' mouths. And of course above all they wanted the utmost discretion, a wall of silence like a lodge of Freemasons sucking dick and taking it up the ass on weekend retreats.

There were the bars and the clubs, the bathhouses, the orgies, the relentless cruising and endless craving, being sated and empty at the same time, speedballing crystal meth with heroin, living it all like the fallen hero in some doped-up crime novel. Quentin Tarantino as Quentin Crisp with a penchant for bondage and camera-ready gore. *What's up with tricks? Tricks are for whores, I'm just playing my cards.*

And then there was Him, the alpha male of his dreams, the all-American rogue who stole poor Cunanan's heart like it was his birthright, the handsome young architect with Ayn Rand in his coat pocket, dreaming trust fund dreams of stately arches and cold granite facades, his destiny laid out big and clear like blueprints to some grand hotel.

So was it just a case of unrequited love? Did you only want him because he told you you were different, not like any of the others? Did he make you feel like you hailed from somewhere else besides Rancho Bernardo? Were you hopeful, chasing down old lovers, thinking things would turn out differently? Did he put you back in your place? In the end, was he the one you couldn't have?

A broken heart, unrequited love, revenge, lust, que dirà que dirà. *All themes are admissible, but nothing is true. There is no story, just a barrage of soundbites, a trail of false leads. You can believe what you want.*

Wasn't it a charmed life after all? What about the stories of the happy-go-lucky playboy, the boisterous bon vivant. You were always a well-kept boy, weren't you? No regrets, no misgivings, untouchable. La la la la. You knew what you were doing all along.

Yeah, I was out in high school, an all-boy's school in La Jolla, where they'd smear your ass just for lisping. But they left me alone. They didn't know what to make of me. I wasn't white, I wasn't a Flip, and I wasn't Mexican.

He sinks into one of his mute spells. I marvel at how his face has aged compared to the boyishly handsome visage in all the magazine photos, and I wonder what his smile would look like now. (I bet it would be one of those sad, fractured smiles, because a coy smile is the smile of a serial killer, and Cunanan—according to the criminologists on CNN—was a spree killer. All the difference, I guess, between a monster and an everyday person driven to monstrous acts).

In a moment of intimacy or maybe distance he'd tell me how it plays out like stills for a movie, *but more overwhelming like pornographic images that flash through your head just before you cum: the look of disbelief and betrayal on his face, how afterwards the same expression remained frozen in his contorted face, his jaw slack, and his eyes black and round as bullet holes. In the garage, the pool of blood indistinguishable from the puddle of car oil, black on black, reflecting the light of a single bare bulb. And just beyond the glare of that single bulb, the real estate developer's body wrapped head-to-toe in duct tape, propped up against the back wall like a silvery mummy.*

I remember hearing about another case, a couple of years ago. I think the guy was from Mississippi. He was closeted, mixed-race, half black, half white. He would stalk his victims at night in public parks and secluded areas where gay men cruised. His victims were exclusively Caucasian men. He would hide in the bushes and then gun them down as they tried to run away. After he was caught, he confessed that it was a failed homosexual love life and his self-hatred that drove him to rampage.

My Filipino father prized his young Americana bride, and maybe I'm just a bitter snow queen. All I know is that after I ran away, I never ceased to be startled by my own reflection. In mirrors in countless motels and reststops, I'd marvel at dull, sunken eyes, the deep creases alongside a thin, expressionless mouth. I'd aged ten years in the same number of months, never to be anybody's boy, ever again. My soul worn away by friction, rubbed off by miles and miles of interstates and byways, I watched it blow away like highway dust.

After a while I stopped hiding, because I knew no one could see me, not even a specter of a shell. I knew that if I just kept driving, eventually the highway would end at these wide,wide black waters-the land on the other side a thin strip low on the horizon. A ferry would come just for me, and I'd drive onboard. As it slowly pulled away, there'd be this song playing on the car radio, one of those love songs with the lush melody piqued by dark brooding lyrics.

II. Libido: Every Good Boy Dutifully Fellates

Of all of the places, the faces, and the towns I've burned into my mind, it's you I find.

My love is like a bullet, it's always true, and it's burning at the heart, and now I've played the part.

Been driving aimlessly through Salt Lake City. The whitest

town in the whole country and I've stumbled upon the sad and ripped back sides where they hide all the Hispanics and poor white trash.

I'm on a mostly commercial strip. Liquor stores, boarded up storefronts. A few more blocks past dark apartments and residential hotels, there's a big yellow marquee, the swarm of letters threatening to buckle off the sign read: *XXX Magazines, Video Arcade, 89 channels, 24 hrs.*

The street out front is empty and there's no one around, but I park halfway down the block past the store. It's almost a full moon, or maybe it's waning. I'm sleepwalking past dark storefronts, ducking in and out of breezeways, avoiding the moonlight.

The glass door and front windows of the shop are painted red from the inside, but at the top corners of the windowpane, the paint is thin and peeling, and there's a glimpse of dusty fluorescent lights chained to a grimy stuccoed ceiling.

I open the door and am blasted by a wall of sickly warm air. At the front counter, an octogenarian with palsy is trying to stick price tags on shrink-wrapped magazines. He doesn't even look up.

I float past a *cloister* of young missionaries in short sleeves and black ties, standing around a magazine rack. They're flipping through dog-eared display copies of big tits and ass and wet splayed pussy. The air is so still that as I walk past, the pages on the racks stir slightly in my wake.

I pass a couple of Mexicans poring over empty video boxes, their brows beaded, their mouths dry and electric with anticipation.

Alone at the gay porno rack a middle-aged househusband admires amateurish photos of smooth eighteen-year-olds.

Scherzo for Cunanan

The entrance to the video arcade is in the far back wall. The doorway is framed by a faded black curtain, tied back midway on either side. The token machine by the doorway sucks up my ten without too much cajoling. The dull bronze tokens that spill out remind me of the video game tokens from the pizza parlors when I was a kid.

Passing through the doorway, I trip the light beam detector, and an electric doorbell sounds. The night watchman standing guard by the entrance gives me a drowsy nod. I've come to realize that all quarter booth joints seem to have the same smell, a composite odor of stale poppers, sweat, cum, and Lysol.

As I reach the first door it opens and I make eye contact with the guy who walks out. He's about my age, maybe thirty at most, the tight drape of his flannel shirt over wide shoulders and a broad chest hinting at a thickly muscled frame. He sports the scruffy, uneven beginnings of a goatee, short-cropped dirty blonde hair, pale eyes. He gives me the kind of stare that tells nothing, no clear sign of lust or loathing or maybe a little of both. I break eye contact and quickly walk past him, suppressing the urge to look back.

The video arcade is an S-shaped labyrinth with doors on either side. There are a few men waiting in the corridor, even though most of the booths are unoccupied. Some of them stand around coolly, scoping out every new arrival. Some shift nervously, eyes darting anxiously, scanning the dim surroundings.

I head straight for a booth near the end of the corridor, pull the door shut behind me, but leave it unlocked. The booth is quite sizable, two fold-up chairs, leg room enough for the lankiest of cowboys to kick back and work up a good hard-on. The side walls are patched with squares of aluminum, probably covering up old glory holes. The monitor is maybe fourteen inches, a blank cyan screen flashing in big white letters: *Insert more tokens.* I put in about fifteen minutes' worth and notice that the screen is actually encased behind a sheet of Plexiglas, smeared with greasy fingerprints and cum shots that have long since crusted over.

The video selection is overwhelming, mostly straight flicks with a smattering of gay porn and girl-on-girl action. I surf through the selection impatiently, looking for the one singular image that'll get me off. Teenage boys masturbate alone and in groups of four or five, in empty warehouses, in hay lofts and forest glens. Two impossibly buxom cinch-waisted white women simultaneously fellate the prodigious cock of a black man, his face stoic as statuary. Hairy daddies impale faceless slaves with fist-sized dildos; the application of lube, the insertion of latexed fingers into accommodating assholes, every gesture calculated and earnest. Smooth, wiry Asian boys, laced up with Japanese knots, writhe on tatami mats. Later, untied, they grind and pivot to a resounding house beat, lathering themselves up with body gel like a pair of Manila macho dancers.

I've surfed through half the channels. Cum shots are few and far between. Either they're barely getting worked up and are far from climaxing, or else someone's coaxing out the last few drops, panting and dreamy-eyed. My fifteen minutes soon run out and I'm feeling uninspired, my cock flaccid.

I hear the clink of tokens being deposited in the next booth. On the wall there's an empty tissue paper dispenser and just below it the beginnings of a glory hole, or rather a peephole, too small to even take a finger. I stoop down to peer through, and if

I stand just right I can barely make out someone's fist squarely grasping the base of his fully erect cock. As he jacks off I can see a wedding band gleaming on his ring finger. I feel my own cock stirring. Without pulling it out, I squeeze the tight form of my cock, taut against the rough denim of my jeans.

I get up to put more tokens in the slot when someone enters my booth. I sit back down trying to calm the sudden surge of blood and adrenaline I can feel coursing through my jugulars. I take my first glance and recognize him as the guy that I cruised when I first entered the arcade. He gives me a quick stiff nod and remains standing, hovering at my side. From my angle his face, which before seemed somewhat angular, now seems puffy as a fratboy's, showing the signs of too many kegs and stoned afternoons. I notice that his belt and half the buttons on his fly are already undone. He pulls the tails of his flannel shirt out, and I catch a glimpse of his belly, a thin downy strip of fur running past a wisp of a belly button down to his crotch.

He tugs at the waistband of his briefs and pulls out an already-half-engorged cock, with a wide, flat shaft, ending in a fat, bulbous head. With his left hand he grips the base of his dick, cinching a couple of fingers around his balls like a makeshift cock ring. With his other hand he caresses the entire vascular length, teasing the swelling head with his fingertips. He inches closer to me so that his cock arches slightly upward toward my face. I turn in my chair to face him and run the tip of my tongue along the sharp fringes of his cockhead. He flinches slightly. I smell the acrid odor from the dark eye of his pisshole. He gestures over to my own swelling member, and before I can oblige, he reaches over, unzips my pants, and pulls out my cock, already glistening with precum.

He backs away a step or two, leaning up against the back corner of the booth. When I reach out to stroke his cock he blocks me with his hand. From his corner he tends to his erection, watching me play with myself and distractedly watching the video screen. There's a straight video playing; the scenario: a conjugal bed, man and wife heatedly consecrating their marriage. She looks yearningly into his eyes as he plows into her.

I find myself recalling the games we used to play. I remember how sometimes as I kneeled to suck you off, I'd look up at you with these sad yearning eyes, forlorn as a whimpering dog or a silverscreen waif (how pathetic I must have looked), then you'd break out of your role and return my gaze, smiling, your brow furrowed in a show of concern, as if to say, yes. Yes, you are my boy, and I want to take care of you.

My cubicle buddy is still leaning up against the back corner, feverishly jacking himself off, his eyes half closed, his lips barely parted. My own hard-on has diminished irretrievably. I tuck myself back in, empty my pockets of any remaining tokens, and place them in a single neat stack on the chair. By the time he realizes I've left, I'm miles and miles away.

III. Resurrection: Cunanan, *Kumain Ka Na*

Andy, my mother told me just before they locked her away in a dark corner of her head, you know there's nothing like a resurrection to put everything right in the world. Have you been going to church, Andy? Rapture's coming soon. Andrew...?

I had imagined that right afterward I'd hear the rattling din of a thousand tiny metal balls of shot rebounding off the walls of my emptied skull, but there is no sound, just an all-consuming burning white heat. Seconds later, or maybe months or years after, this white heat, this notion of nuclear fission burns out, fizzles to a deep celestial droning. Psychic residue: Random flashes and sparks die out against a deadened retina. Slowly the deep droning fades from a sound to a color or a suggestion of color barely discernible from the void. The color grows in intensity till it's a warm red shell held together by bloody tendrils. The red sheath gives way to a flurry of sunspots, and the sunspots dissipate to reveal the same threatening blue sky hanging over the same familiar highways and back roads. Maybe there's kudzu vines strangling telephone lines or eating into the soft shoulders of the interstate; maybe bright poisonous flowers bloom in the highway median; or maybe it's the tortured landscape of the badlands, all menacing rocks and angry crags.

Maybe I'm the second coming, on the third day, unfiled from my drawer in the county morgue—but I'm no Jesus Christ; my mother may be sainted, but no one prays to her, and God the Father couldn't be a Filipino.

Maybe it's not an afterlife, not a life at all, but just going through the motions, just driving and driving, the wind through the open windows pulsing in my ears like the warbling of seraphim.

But there is one thing I am certain of: I know that you're dead. I know because I've killed you a thousand times over in my dreams alone.

So now I drive alone and all roads lead west, and I find I'm headed back to the city, the city I called home for seven years. San Francisco, number-one tourist destination in the country, sanctuary to madmen of all persuasions: poets, artists, musicians, murderers. The final destination for all lost souls and vanquished identities. So went the legend from the old Barbary Coast: The legions of the vanished and the forgotten eventually resurfaced in San Francisco.

I wonder if people will still recognize me, old friends and acquaintances I haven't seen in years? Will anyone still consider me part of their fold? The truest test of loyalty: be publicly accused of committing a killing spree and assassinating one of the most celebrated, arguably the most idolized, fashion designers of our time, a veritable gay hero, and then see who still counts you as one of their own. *Versace, Versace, now that you've gone, your house will live on and on.*

I'm sure only my Libra friends will still stand by me, but I suppose they're only loyal by default, and if they were born under any other sign they'd probably curse my name like everyone else has, admitting that they knew me once or thought they knew me, shaking their heads in disbelief.

We thought you were dead, they'd say, thinking I looked like shit, the living dead right before their disapproving eyes, their lips pursed in disparagement.

I did die, I'd tell them, I've died and gone to hell, and I guess I made it to the very bottom, because there's no one here but back-stabbing traitors.

San Franciscans, of all people, should know to be wary of what they read or hear. After all, isn't this where William Randolph Hearst unleashed his fledgling newspaper, a rag notorious for peddling all manner of apocrypha and shameless sensationalism? In the public eye you are reduced to a sketch, a height, a skin tone, a dossier of tabloid clippings, a biography pieced together from hearsay and the basest of deductive logic. Maybe people need to believe in monsters: pedophiles, vampires, serial killers-a twisted reaffirmation of their belief in their own humanity and goodwill, their faith in God.

So what do they want to hear? That I went to an all-boys prep school with the sons of millionaires? That my father spoiled his half-white son? He told me before he disappeared across the sea that my mother's blood would save me, that I would be entitled to everything I surveyed and would never have to trudge through life with the untouchable and the unseen.

Should I tell them it was preordained that between the ages of twenty-three and twenty-six, I would fall in love with a succession of older lovers, every one a model of gentility? That with the best of my lovers I was worthy of everything I surveyed? That I was indeed well kept, and always had been?

Should I tell them how when I first saw him I claimed him with my eyes, because I was taught to believe that I could? How I always felt safe and everything was always in its place when I was with him? How everyone in his circle of friends and colleagues respected him, how when I first pondered the idea that someone could bring him down, it wrecked all my notions of Order?

Maybe they want to hear that I've never had a sense of place, that I've always felt that no one could claim me as kin, and that I've always believed in the myth of the open road, the promise of western skies. That I grounded myself in him, and when he left me, I lost all sense of belonging that I ever had. That maybe I went looking for him to retrieve what I was never willing to relinquish. And maybe I had it all mapped out. Things would work out just so, and maybe my faith, my desire, were so unrelenting that everything afterward fragmented and dissolved.

Maybe I blocked everything out, a singular motion, nothing to catalogue but landscapes and miles and miles of steely asphalt. Maybe holed up in some motor lodge in West Palm Beach, staring in the vanity mirror at my haggard reflection, I suddenly knew what my lot in life was. I discovered a supreme fiction: The only way to rectify such iniquity is to tear away, set asunder, the spurious sense of order, the easy target of craven flesh and fallen idols, watch the buildings fall away and the people disappear, a ghostly world, a dead country.

I've parked the car at the Cliff House, the northwest corner of the city. I've left the headlights on and they beam out over the cliff's edge, illuminating the eddies of sea spray wafting up from the shore. In the darkness below, nestled between the cliff walls are the modern-day ruins of the Sutro baths, a huge complex of indoor pools that fell to disrepair and finally burned to the ground, nothing left but concrete basins full of stagnant algae-infested waters.

I imagine I see a figure running recklessly fast along the dirt trail that descends in a single wide sweeping arc down to the ruins below. I imagine it's me. My silhouette disappears against the dark thickets of wild blackberry brambles that threaten to overtake the path. It reappears at the other end, the edge of the first basin, running atop the narrow, jagged surface of broken walls, paying no heed to the exposed rebar that threatens to pierce a misplaced foot. The figure safely reaches the last wall just before the shore and leaps down to the wet sands, arms flailing behind him, then he runs straight into the cold Pacific, his head lost amidst the white crests of breaking waves. What I imagine to be my drowned body floating in the shallow wash is really just a piece of driftwood brought in by the tide.

Dusting for Fingerprints

Andrew Spieldenner

It was the flowers every Saturday she anticipated. Oh, sure, Christina Sanchoun loved to see her son. He was easily everything his father wanted—better educated and higher paid than the previous generation, deferential to his father in most conversations and, though the old man would never admit it, good-looking. If it weren't for the homosexuality, Christina was sure she'd never hear the end of their perfect son Raul.

Weekly, Christina managed the two trains she had to take to have coffee and bread with him. Inescapably neat, the apartment, except for minor additions like the latest photo book, had looked the same for four years. He could have sent a photo to *Better Homes & Gardens*, or, if such a magazine existed, *Geometric Rentals for Singles with Taste.* Even the Warhol diptych made sense above the silver-edged glass table, behind the restored gray, thick-tasseled couch. She brought fresh bread from the French bakery near her Queens home. He made coffee—strong, sweet, rich.

They spend the time in easy poses. Chats about day-to-day occurrences: newest changes with the cats, the ailments of age entering her or her husband, how work goes on and on, gossip about cousins and aunts, old family friends who went back to the Philippines, that recent funny TV special or shocking movie.

Christina does not like to read anymore. The Bible in her purse she only picks at to make her faith appear complete. She wishes sometimes to bring up her dreams-what she wanted Raul to be, what she still dreams of him doing. Instead she tells him she is proud of him and glad for his happiness. It's important to Raul. She has seen MTV's "Real World" and the afternoon specials on gay children.

Raul, for his part, enjoys these poses without discussions of love and lovers, without mentioning the pain each has wrapped in ornate gold rings. Fingers grip his beloved Beverly Hillbilly mugs a trifle too tightly.

Raul thinks of appropriate moments to share with his mother, to make these visits like a string of International Coffee memories. The idea that his life could be a commercial entrances him. It helps block out last night, the man's smell returning with odd turns of the head. The odor of his balls especially.

Johnny-something, Raul thought. It had been a dark bar, a drunken evening, and Johnny looked quiet. Clean for a Lower East Side blonde. His hair was longer than Raul liked, hanging just over his right eye. He had come up to Raul with an extra beer and a crooked smile. His tight jeans were ripped at the left knee. He wasn't wearing underwear and his thin prick stood out. His denim shirt, even with erratic wash stains, was ironed. Three thin black rubber bracelets fell just below his wrist. Johnny's fingers held the bottle's neck gently.

"Oh Mother, remember the Christmas you had the bike waiting for me in the kitchen? I almost caught you and Dad setting it up. You dragged me back to bed and lectured me about surprising Santa Claus. That bike made my eyes sparkle like a star. Do you remember?"

She remembers working overtime hours at the office, saving

money, choosing a bike Raul would love, carrying it home on the subway, afraid of getting mugged. Alone, without any assistance, she did this for him. Raul immediately leapt to his father with a hug, giggling, full of gratitude for a man who grunted his approval. His father had not bothered to look at the bike, had barely gotten up to demand breakfast. Christina was already working on lumpia, rice, ham, collard greens, candied yams, and pumpkin pie. She was still learning American Christmas cooking.

That was a bad year. Raul had been beaten up twice by the neighborhood kids, his teacher complained about his accent, and he had few phone calls or friends. None of this bothered his father until he noticed Raul steadily becoming more girlish. Or at least that's how he described the boy's actions and moods to Christina. Preferring home life and libraries, helping with cleaning and interested in the proper use of spices, pots, pans. Preferring solitude and books, singing softly to ballads in his room, the companionship of his mother and the occasional girl from school. Christina noticed what no one else did, how handsome Raul was growing, how perfectly he meshed her cheekbones and light brown with his father's full lips and pointed nose. To Christina, Raul glowed with promise.

Johnny stammered, "I, uh, saw you were alone. I mean, did you come here with anyone?"

"No. You were right. I came alone."

"Do you have plans? I mean, you must be meeting people later, right?"

"No. I'm not."

They both smiled because they each had nothing else to say. Raul accepted Johnny's beer, lightly brushing the thin rubber bands.

Christina had been anxious to get to the U.S., to the new life awaiting her. She had wanted to be a respected writer, her own kind of Hemingway or Twain, when she was in high school. She had thought: maybe not on these islands, but in America, there is freedom. And with these thoughts kissing her lips softly, gloriously, she found a man likely to move, seduced him, and endured years of marriage for their migration.

She twists her wedding band slowly.

The local community college had no place for her, no classes for people with no f's in their language and too much Spanish in their names. That's what the '70s were like for her and she never understood claims otherwise. Sure there were a lot of brown people going to class, but a lot dropped out. Even Christina Sanchoun, who had envisioned her name on book covers and dreamed her presence would be required, like James Baldwin's, for appearances on television special reports. But she had a child to raise, a husband who could not cook, no family, a data entry job to find, no friends to watch her baby, no classes to accommodate her thick accented English, and her quiet belief in her own views.

When he threatened to divorce her and send her back with Raul, she dropped the class. In America, she would be a good, if dispassionate, wife, and a driven, accurate mother and data entry clerk.

She twists her ring as if dirt is rubbing away beneath it.

Outside the bar, Johnny kissed with his whole mouth, his lips parted wide to swallow Raul's face entirely. Johnny's lips were too thin, forming a slit in his face. Their tongues fought rudely, making Raul thoroughly uncomfortable. He had an erection and there was still a steady bustle of couples and hooligans sharing the street corner. Johnny closed his eyes while kissing; Raul didn't.

"Um, let's get off the street," Raul whispered sheepishly.

"OK. You got some place in mind? I got roommates," Johnny confessed, his crooked smile just starting.

Raul hailed a taxi.

"Oh Raul, you always were an easy boy to please," Christina tries to sound light-hearted, like a supportive mother, "Each gift was a pleasure."

"Oh Mom," responds Raul, confused at the insult he almost hears, "you've been the best. How's Dad?"

"Oh, he still gets around," Christina says a little too loud and thinks, *Still makes it to all those strip bars and fondles those women's breasts, thank God.*

Raul sees his parents as happy together. Overjoyed.

Christina believed in justice for a long time. She thought it powerful, capable of making her toes clench, entering through her like love-tough, fearless, unforgiving. Watching Raul grow into a man his father could be proud of, a man she was sure everyone adored, wore down her belief. Where was his curiosity? Why did he never ask about her life, her family's life, what she had left in the Philippines? The books she had given him over the years had been lost somewhere in his moves. *Go Tell It On the Mountain. This Bridge Called My Back. China Men. Meridian.* All lost somewhere in the rooms he called home.

She stares out the window. They are on the fourth floor. The sky is still bright. Morning traffic has picked up since her arrival.

It was hardest to remain quiet with a tongue sliding in and out of his ass. But Johnny had Raul stomach down, legs spread, back curved, tight butt perched high. Raul pushed his face further into the pillow. He tried to block the sounds of Johnny slurping, licking, nibbling his smooth skin.

Johnny, for his part, didn't stop. He moved too hurriedly, yanking off his pants. He gnawed on Raul's hard, smooth ass, licking the small, tender balls dangling before him. He threw Raul over and sucked hard on his penis.

Raul wanted him to stop. He wanted to kiss Johnny again before cock tainted his small lips. But it was too late. So he grabbed the back of Johnny's head, wrapping blonde hair around his knuckles. He pushed up and shoved Johnny back. He fucked Johnny's mouth, trying to keep him silent.

Johnny licked and sucked awkwardly, sometimes using teeth. Raul squirmed, but never said "Be gentle." Johnny started making noises. Raul pulled his dick out and slapped him across the mouth with it. Slapped him again before shoving it back in. Raul clenched his eyes shut; his balls slammed against Johnny's rough chin. Johnny held Raul's butt, and slowly slipped a single finger in.

This week Christina dreamed about her son flying. He was soaring higher and higher, and his voice was heard by many. It trembled, showing vulnerability and honesty. He was singing about his hope, her past and his hope blended. He was beautiful in her dream and everyone felt it, could see the truth of their lives for the first time, and it made her weep. She woke with the tears drying on her cheeks. Her husband said nothing, never brought up her sobbing in her sleep.

Raul sips his coffee. His mother, hair carefully held with hair spray, gold at her ears and around her neck, right wrist, and left finger, sat smiling. Raul glowed in her eyes. He could tell.

When he was in design school, she had stopped by twice a week, bringing homemade food and snacks. These visits made Raul the hit of his dorm. His mother, friendly with his friends, always asked about the week's events. She was by far the most concerned and understanding parent of all. She even brought books over, at least once a month. Raul found it adorable and thanked her genuinely, each time. Even if those books were nowhere in his courses. He didn't want her to feel useless. He tried to be supportive.

Raul's design school friends still ask about her.

Raul smelled him and could think of no way to block it. Unshowered, Johnny was all sour sweat and cigarettes. Especially on his balls. Raul was sitting on Johnny's fingers, two inside him, stifling his groan, trying not to look at Johnny's erect prick, leaning up at him, pleading. Raul fell forward on the bed, down Johnny's body, giving Johnny's fingers better entry. Each push into him made Raul want to cry. He could smell Johnny.

Raul writhed against Johnny's hand. Johnny's dick, thin like his lips, stark white against surprising auburn pubic hair, got close to Raul's face. It touched him. Raul sucked on Johnny's nuts. Johnny moaned and pushed his fingers faster. Harder.

Face deep in groin, Raul licked. He shifted his ass in beat to Johnny's fingers. Raul hated this awful violation, despised the wonder of penetrating fingers. He wanted to forget Johnny's fingers. Raul was submerged in Johnny's pungent crotch. His teeth scraped Johnny's tender balls.

Defying Raul, Johnny let loose a groan. The hum vibrated along Raul's dick, still filling Johnny's mouth. Raul had firmly shut his eyes again. Raul's butt was warm and tight. It swallowed Johnny' fingers obediently, almost eagerly. Johnny's balls tingled.

Johnny, thin and pink-white, strained inside Raul. Raul's small, muscled frame glistened while he moved his hips around, further onto Johnny's fingers. Raul liked the contrast of his natural brown skin, his sculpted, smooth chest and abs, his ass and legs above Johnny. Raul overpowered Johnny.

Raul wanted to shut Johnny up. He steadily stroked Johnny. Touched his balls quick and rough. Raul slammed his ass further onto Johnny's fingers, now three, opening up. He breathed sex, yet refused to believe he wanted it—that he was hungry too.

Raul's hand clenched Johnny's dick, slid up and down in synch with his own ass. He licked Johnny's balls quick and rough like a cat. Held his swollen prick. He was on top of Johnny. Raul surrounded him. Johnny bit Raul's foot.

Raul was hard, and smiled. Johnny was silent, mouthing the curve between heel and toes. Raul almost groaned. He stroked harder. Faster. He took Johnny's pungent balls in his mouth, his teeth scraping. He nuzzled against Johnny's thighs and the inside part between balls and ass. Raul's butt writhed.

Raul slammed his ass hard. Fast. Smooth skin massaging Johnny's wiry fur. He licked and stroked. Precum and sweat lubricated Johnny's chest. Raul's ass tightened. His dick burst. He came.

Seconds later, so did Johnny.

He kissed Johnny's balls.

Christina watches her son's face. He is recounting some banal encounter with a sales clerk this week, or a cab driver, or a corner store owner. Every week, he fills the space between them with these small facts. She endures it, smiling.

Christina remembers whispering large dreams into those ears. Her son would not live like she did; he would be free. There was a time, when he explained his homosexuality, that she dared hope those prayers meant something. Now, she looks around his apartment-too neat, sterile even-sips her strong, deep coffee, dips her bread and chews. She has these Saturday mornings with him. And they mean so much to him.

She looks out the window. Outside, sun shines. People rush around the city, on their way to see someone, to find evidence of their dreams.

Sunday

Dan Taluapapa McMullin

There was a seminary student from Samoa. His parents escorted him to Minnesota. He was the first Samoan Lutheran seminary student. There are Mormons, Catholics, Congregationalists all over Samoa. But he was the first Lutheran. His parents stood on either side of him in the middle of Nicolett Mall on a summer day. In the same spot where Mary Tyler Moore threw her hat into the air.

The Reverend Knarffssen came out of his cathedral at the north end of the mall. Approaching the three Polynesians he suddenly smiled. Winter was so far away. Somewhere among the gargoyles. "Such warm, happy people," was his first thought.

"I shall treat Pali as I treat my own son, the assistant reverend," the Reverend Knarffssen told Mr. and Mrs. Saolefaleoteinemauga, taking Pali's moist brown hand and touching it to his dry cheek.

Mr. and Mrs. Saolefaleoteinemauga beamed smiles like tropic birds floating slowly across their high faces: Mr. Saolefaleoteinemauga staunch as the sides of Savaii and Mrs. Saolefaleoteinemauga a single column of devotion and prayer. "Take care of our boy." Pali, six foot five, looked down at the five-foot-five Reverend.

"I will," said the Reverend, and lowered his head in a few words of thanksgiving while his eyes traced the ascending lines of Pali's thighs.

Summer in Minnesota was hot and green. Then, as happens annually in Minnesota during the third week of October, winter descended swiftly with snow and ice.

Christmas came and went. Pali was invited to spend part of winter break with the Reverend Knarffssen and his son Gregg, the assistant pastor. Pali wondered about the rumor that Gregg and the Reverend were not actually related by blood but by common interest, as he noted the difference in physical appearance during the first sauna the three of them took together.

In fact, the three of them were sitting naked in the Pastor's basement within fifteen minutes of Pali's arrival, coming into the house after the drive from the seminary in town with Gregg. The Pastor, bounding down the stairs in his bathrobe, invited Pali to join them for their afternoon invigorating Swedish sauna. Before you could say, *Uff da!*, Pali was on a high pine bench pouring spring water from a wooden dipper, watching eucalyptus-scented steam rise between him and his nude hosts. Pali wore a towel, having been brought up a modest Christian Samoan.

"I would have thought that being Polynesian," said the Pastor, plumbing his bottomless well of ignorance, "you wouldn't have hangups about nudity and such things."

"We were brought up never to swim on Sundays and always to wear a T-shirt to the beach," answered Pali.

"Oh, how we must have fucked you poor bastards up the ass," moaned the Pastor, standing on floor level and looking into the shadow under Pali's towel, thinking of missionaries.

Pali took a moment to ponder this. His embarrassment at the casual nudity forced him to keep his eyes above the Pastor's jawline, and he refused to acknowledge Pastor

Knarffssen's erection. From the Pastor's pale, boyish body, with its slim hips and small ass, there curving upward toward his chest a great fat colorless prick that glistened around the head as precum dribbled onto the blond floor. "Actually most of the Christian missionaries to Samoa came from Rarotonga," was Pali's response.

The Pastor tweaked the head of his prick, making it pink, and coated the round shaft with a palm full of stuff. The smallness of the Pastor's torso made the long curve of his hard-on all the more incredible. But Pali's discretion was boundless. Even a stiff dick with a heartbeat, trembling between his ankles in the steam, would not alter his respectful attention to his mentor's words.

The Pastor sat down on the bench at Pali's feet with a sigh. "Gregg, why don't you do your exercises?" he suggested. Gregg was not immune to the charms of the Pastor's member-it was the Pastor's one physically alluring quality. But today, he felt shy around Pali. Rather than taking the Pastor's hidden cue, he began instead to actually exercise.

Gregg started with stretches. He sat on the high bench opposite Pali. Spreading his legs, he touched his fingers to the tips of his toes. The sauna was quiet with only the sound of Gregg's breathing and the creaking bench—and Pastor Knarffssen's yanking. Gregg and the Pastor together glanced at the dark brown nipples on Pali's broad chest softening in the heat.

Pali looked curiously at Gregg. He was as tall as Pali and as broad shouldered. While the Pastort was narrow, Gregg had thick thighs and a jutting, dimpled ass, perfectly round. While the Pastor was covered in invisible white hairs that tickled anyone he sat by, Gregg was a smooth slab of corn-fed farm boy. "They're not related at all," Pali decided.

"Oh, flex that ass," muttered the Pastor watching his assistant.

"This reminds me of Fiji," said Pali.

"Why Fiji?" asked the Pastor.

"I used to go swimming with the Catholic seminarians there-this was before I decided to study the teachings of Martin Luther," said Pali.

"Where'd you swim?" asked the Pastor.

"At a waterfall near Suva. Once a Tongan woman from New Zealand joined us, she said she was a writer; we could see her breasts under her wet lavalava, and she said all sorts of suggestive things!"

"Like what?" asked the Pastor.

"I made hors d'oeuvres!" said Gregg, jumping up and running out of the sauna.

"My son is nervous today," said the Pastor. "You'd think it was the first time we've had a guest from overseas."

The snow was ripping through the air outside. Pali stood in the master bedroom wearing a lavalava that the Pastor had given him. "I've bought one for each of us! They're Polynesian pareos," said the Pastor.

"It looks Malaysian," Pali said, noting the paisley patterns.

"So it's true they don't wear anything underneath?" said the Pastor, rubbing his eyebrow, looking down at his tent.

"Suits the climate," said Pali, "I can't seem to find any of my clothes right now."

"Probably in the laundry," said the Pastor, "We always try to get the visitors' effects immediately into the wash. Seminarians!" The Pastor tried pressing his hard-on against Pali's hipbone.

Pali felt only *ava*, *faaaloalo*, and *alofa mo le toeaina:* respect, reverence, and love for one's elder. He found the Minnesota Lutheran clergyman's home life exotic. He went down the stairs and into the carpeted living room. The Pastor, chasing after him, tucked the hem of his pareo into the waistband, his now shrinking but still swollen member tossing up and about.

"Pali! Pali! I just want to chat!" shouted the Pastor, as Pali dodged the oak furniture and scattered Pastor Knarffssen's extensive collection of wooden craft items. Knocking over an elmwood rabbit, Pali raced through the kitchen and out onto the sundeck. The snow was now flying about in big wet flakes, hitting Pali's black hair and smooth back. Like footballers in training, Pali and the Pastor ran high stepping around the house through the deep, icy prairie grass.

Pali came around to the front door and went in, slamming it behind him, locking it and drawing the chain. The Pastor shook the doorknob angrily; after all, it was his home. He got the key from under the planter and unlocked the door, but the chain stopped him, "Oh gall darn, you went and did it!" he shouted. Pali watched garden clippers snip through the imitation brass door chain, then walked back up the stairs to another bedroom, closing the latch on the bedroom doorknob.

He was in his guest room. Gregg lay on his bed with his face in the pillow, his legs spread in a *V*-shape toward Pali. Gregg turned around and asked, "Would you like to smoke? I bet the

Pastor decides to watch TV. He's like that, exists from one moment to the next."

It was quiet in the house. Pali could hear a Vikings football pregame talk show on the TV from the living room. He sat on the bed next to Gregg. "I made sushi for ya," said Gregg.

"Ah?" said Pali, taking some rolls from the hors d'oeuvres plate.

"Well it's really California roll made with lefsa."

"It's good," said Pali, eating another palmful.

Gregg lit a joint and pulled a box of poppers and lube from the drawer. "We probably seem pushy to ya?" asked Gregg, before holding his breath and then blowing smoke into Pali's lungs. "It's my dang Dad, he acts like a kid sometimes."

"The chasing reminds me of kids," said Pali.

Gregg put aside the smoke and pushed Pali down, their tongues entangling like crazed flags. In reply, Pali pulled Gregg onto himself. He ran his palms down Gregg's curved back into his pareo, caressing his asscheeks. Gregg swiveled and ground his chest into Pali's; Pali pinched Gregg's nipples between his thumbs and forefingers. From beneath, Pali humped Gregg's groin with his own, and through their pareos their cocks tracked and slipped. Gregg's tongue beat against Pali's lips, nostrils, bridge, eyelids, into his ear, along his shoulder, into his armpit, inside his elbow, into his pareo and finally, led by the veins, brought Pali's dick into his mouth, and slicked the cock with his spit.

Pali balanced on his elbow in the bed and turned Gregg's body around, as they each pulled the pareo from the other's body, and each fucked their cocks into the other's mouth. Pali slid on top and, arching from the root, sent the tip of his prick beyond

Gregg's throat muscle, forcing him to control his breath. Gregg hummed into the head of Pali's dick. They turned and turned back on the bed, again and again, without releasing each other. The Vikings game played out downstairs, and the Pastor tossed in his chair, thinking of yet another guest one-on-one with Gregg.

Gregg pushed Pali back on the bed, his knees on either side of Pali's waist. He pressed his asshole onto Pali's standing dick and took it slowly in. Gregg's cock branched hard into Pali's sliding fist. Each inner ring of his ass opened until Pali's cock was buried deep inside. Pali's stroking blurred. Gregg's cum shot onto the wall beside the bed and ran down Pali's wrist.

Pali took Gregg's legs in his arms and brought Gregg belly down onto the bed, arching his hips into Gregg's clutching cheeks. Pali's face was empty like a runner's. Gregg's groans carried into the living room. Pali came inside Gregg's smooth, shaking ass. Then he kissed Gregg's thick shoulders, pressed his face against Gregg's, and closed his eyes.

"Our wives will be coming back from their shopping trip to Chicago tonight. It's only been a weekend, but I miss the grandchildren!" said the Pastor at breakfast the next morning. Pali watched Gregg, who was working the Sunday crossword puzzle. Before you could say, *Kafefe!* Pali was back on the freeway headed toward the towers of the Twin Cities. This time the Pastor himself drove him. Gregg stayed home, trying to repair a bicycle for one of his young daughters.

"You know, it's about time Gregg took on his own parish," said the Pastor in the car. "I'm thinking of a really nice place I know near Moscow, Minnesota."

Pali was entertaining thoughts of becoming a Buddhist. He'd met some Tibetan monks at a doll store in Stillwater. Minnesota has the largest Tibetan population in the U.S., they'd told him. "Oh what shame I will bring to my family, if I return to Samoa without a degree in Lutheran divinity!" thought Pali to himself. "Better to hide myself in this place forever, become a prostitute or a computer programmer." What other work had the seminary trained him for?

Pastor Knarffssen noted Pali's distraction and suggested they stop outside Minneapolis-St. Paul Airport to watch the jets take off. They sat silently together in the Pastor's car, parked within the repair yard fence. The planes taxied one at a time up to a turning mark near their viewpoint. Rumbling, the aircraft raced onto the field. Watching, Pali decided he would finish out the years of study he had begun, marry a nice Samoan Lutheran, build himself a Swedish sauna near Apia. He leaned back to watch the planes through the sunroof. One by one, he felt them shudder into the air and vanish.

True Love

Nino Alvarez

1.

Sam followed the pattern of pubic hair that ran across Merrill's belly. The brown skin of his naked torso rose and fell in soft mounds like a gentle landscape. The line of fine hairs came to an invisible point somewhere deep in his lover's belly button, resembling a flock of crows heading south for the winter. Sam couldn't resist the urge to plunge his finger into his lover's navel.

"What are you doing, Sam, I was 'sleep," Merrill moaned.

"Dinnertime." Sam narrowed his tongue and drill dove into the warm linty depths of his lover's belly hole. He was met with Merrill's familiar musk and strangely enough a slight underscore of peppermint.

"Dinnertime for who, me or you?" Merrill chuckled. "I am starved!"

Sam looked up and deduced from the familiar dents in Merrill's short afro and the faint, powdery line that ran from his mouth to the side of his cheeks that Merrill had been asleep for most of the afternoon. Sam felt warm all over knowing that he kept Merrill in such luxury, he was able to take afternoon naps whenever he wanted. It should always be this way for his baby.

"We're having Chinese tonight," Sam said in sing-song.

"Did you cook?"

"You know my mother never taught me how, and if she ever decides to get on a plane, you will never forget what Hong

Kong Cuisine is all about."

Sam knew that his mother would never cook for his lover. Sam also knew that with the death of his father five years ago, the chance of her ever leaving Vancouver was buried along with him. Like a dutiful son, he sent his aging mother and his sister Mei a handsome monthly allowance. Mrs. Chang loved her son and thought him perfect. A San Francisco computer programmer. Handsome. Generous. Obedient.

Mrs. Chang's only disappointment was that she was not able to find a good wife for her son. Admittedly, she never tried as hard as other Chinese mothers might have. Why Mrs. Liu, a nice lady from her temple, did everything from consulting a matchmaker to spending a small fortune sending young Chinese girls from Hong Kong just so that her fragile-boned son could deny each and every girl he was offered. What an embarrasment he was! Mrs. Liu and the other women from her temple blamed it on Western ways. No, Mrs. Chang didn't make much of a fuss. Besides, she liked knowing that she was the only important woman in her son's life. And Mei was happy enough to receive her brother's generous monthly allowance. It allowed her to pursue her painting career that had not yet blossomed. She never felt particularly close to her brother, but she recognized that the money he sent regularly was adequate to keep her from the mundane distractions of a regular job. Mei was quite content with her life. So much so that she never threatened to visit him in San Francisco and ask questions regarding his personal life.

Sam imagined that if his mother could get past the fact that his lover was a man, she might actually bcome quite fond of Merrill. Well, on second thought she would also have to get past the fact that Merrill was African-American. And there would certainly be a lot of explaining regarding his appearance.

Despite the raging hard-on pressing against the side of his slacks, he pulled himself away from his lover's softness to unload the quickly cooling paper food containers from the plastic sacks. For dinner tonight, he had chosen butterfly shrimp, green onion pancakes, barbeque spare ribs and the egg rolls Merrill loved so much. Hot and sour was the soup of the day and Sam was sure to remind the proprietor, who was also the chef, to make his order with extra pork. The main courses consisted of General Tso's chicken, mongolian beef, shrimp in lobster sauce, and the house special, fried rice. Sam made sure to get two orders of the special lo mein and egg foo young for Merrill's breakfast. The same chef/proprietor, thankful for Sam's loyalty, never had to be reminded to place his favorite customer before all other orders and every dish was packed in the micro-pails that Sam preferred. The micro-pails were actually for Merrill's convenience. It pained Sam to think that his lover might have to struggle to prepare a meal for himself. He wanted to be the one to warm his lover's food and whenever possible he preferred to feed his lover himself. He didn't want his lover to have to do anything but concentrate on their project. Sam was comforted that it was only a few more weeks until he was allowed to work from his house. He wanted to keep constant watch over his lover's progress.

From a separate bag, Sam removed a rectangular aluminum dish that contained his customary steamed broccoli with chicken breast. He was careful to measure a proportionate amount of breast to broccoli in order to comply with his training regimen.

Sam caught his reflection in the mirror and liked what he saw. His open shirt showed the six pack that he struggled each morning to better define. His aim was to achieve a physique like Bruce Lee's, except with a bit more bulk. Sam was relatively short for an American-born Chinese, but that didn't stop him from pursuing his ideal of a perfect body.

For tonight's ambiance, Sam lit at least a dozen candles and placed them around the bed. He turned off all the lights in his loft and the soft candlelight glowed around his lover's king-sized bed. At his last weigh-in, Merrill finally pushed the three hundred mark and Sam started to prepare for his lover's journey to the four hundred mark. He figured that it would take at least another year or two to get Merrill to the half-ton mark-the ultimate goal.

From the kitchen area, Merrill's stomach called for dinner. The growl reminded Sam of a tribal percussion or a jungle animal passing gas. He hastened his preparation so that his lover wouldn't have to wait a minute longer. Merrill, his angel, was helpless and starved.

Sam placed each open carton on a rolling cart and moved it to his lover's bedside. He stripped to his drawers and proceeded to seat himself beside his lover. When they first met, Merrill was resistant to Sam feeding him but after a while he merely succumbed to Sam's will. Sam convinced Merrill that this was how he demonstrated his love, and that he expected nothing less than Merrill's total compliance as a reciprocation of his affections.

After the appetizer course and the soup, Sam laid aside the spoon he had been using to shovel heaps of vegetable, meat, and gravy into Merrill's mouth. Using his fingers, Sam retrieved three large asteroid-shaped pieces of General Tso's chicken and held them with his teeth. He lowered his face to Merrill's and with grease-slicked fingers he began to rub Merrill's right nipple to life. Simultaneously, he dropped the chicken pieces into Merrill's gaping mouth like a mother bird to a chick. Sam's thick, purple cock poked out of his briefs and dribbled along the cottage cheese sides of Merrill's belly, which rose and fell like a sleeping beast. As Merrill chewed, Sam slipped his cock between the pocket of fat under what was once a chin and his padded breastbone. A thin film of sweat lubricated his slow glide and he imagined that this was how soft a young girl's thighs must feel.

2.

They met at a cafe. It was the neutral thing to do. Lavelle, Merrill's best friend and second cousin, finally convinced him to post an ad on the internet personals and some guy named Sam was the first to leave an e-mail. When Merrill finally pulled together enough courage to call him, he was both pleased and surprised to find that Sam was as inexperienced at personal ads as he was. Once they got past the initial nervousness, Merrill offered him his phone number.

Sam was quick to put Merrill at ease by making sure he knew that Sam was really listening and really interested in other things besides the fact that he was black. Merrill hadn't met anyone quite like Sam. Most of the time, white men had approached him brimming with Mandingo fantasies. Merrill has definitely had his share of white men. It was actually quite refreshing to meet another man of color.

Merrill couldn't imagine being with another black man. It seemed too much like incest. Despite the attention other black men paid him, he was resistant to their charms. Judging from the bad lines and the occasional hoots he would get on the street or from passing cars, he was quite aware that his ass was his greatest asset. Merrill had always had a large behind, so much so that when he was younger his mother would tease him and claim that his ass stuck out so far she could set a drink on it. Oh, he's heard them all. *Hey man, yo bootie is all on yo' back. Uh-hey man yo ass is so big it takes up two zip codes.* On some level, they were meant to be compliments but he never took them as such. To make matters worse, Merrill grew up always feeling fat. Whenever his mama would sense his discomfort regarding his weight, she just reminded him that he was "thick." And being thick meant that he was healthy.

From Oakland's China Hill it takes approximately twenty to twenty-five minutes to drive over the Bay Bridge and into downtown San Francisco. Merrill has not spoken to his mother nor has he had contact with anyone else in his family for ten years. Well, except Lavelle. But he's a second cousin and that doesn't count. Unlike Lavelle, Merrill's God-fearing mother could neither allow nor condone a faggot in her life, especially her only son. Merrill can still remember the hell he caught when Mrs. Lavetta Jenkins, a devout Seventh Day Adventist, accidentally slipped one of her boy's dirty tapes into the VCR. She almost died right there. He moved out that same evening and now almost ten years later, he still has not exchanged a single word with his mother nor anyone else from the Jenkins God-fearing clan. Merrill's apartment faced the Bay Bridge and on some nights, he swore that he could see straight into his mother's window.

"Lavelle, would you please go home. I'll be fine."

"Uh-uh girl, I want to see this Chinese man you bagged. Ms. One, you better find out if what they say about...you know...is true."

"No, I don't know, and that stereotype is fucked up. And what did I tell you about calling me girl...and in public?" Merrill was clearly annoyed as he stirred his latté nervously. Suddenly, he was panicked. He regretted ordering a coffee drink. His breath was going to reek! What if this guy kissed him? Oh what was his name...Sam?

"Chill out, *girl!* And when did you get so politically correct, and if I can remember correctly you're the black man who wouldn't give another black man nooch!"

"It's not like that, Lavelle." This never-ending argument was torture for Merrill. He was praying that Lavelle would just leave well enough alone.

"It's not like that?" Lavelle mocked. So much for leaving well enough alone. Lavelle unseated his thin frame and proceeded to stand. There was going to be some church up in here. Lavelle took his right index finger and waved it menacingly at Merrill's face like a witch doctor's wand.

"Oh no, Ms. Thing? What is it like then? Let me tell you something. I don't know what it's gonna take for you to get over this white obsession you got. Remember sweet sister cousin, it was me who moved your black ass out of two fucked-up relationships. Two crackers who kicked your ass on a regular basis and two cracker asses I had to kick and you still chasin' after white dick."

Merrill was praying for a miracle. He looked out the window to see if God might be kind enough to send a lightning bolt Lavelle's way so that he would finally shut up! But no such luck. The read continued.

"I shoulda let yo, dumb ass stay in with those white men. I told you that you needed to get with a brother who will treat you right. But noooooo.... So, maybe a Latino man or a Chinese man, anybody else with a little more color. Is that too much to ask? Whatever girl, you are hopeless. I got to go." Disgusted, Lavelle dramatically swept his coat over his shoulders. Looking over at the table, Merrill caught sight of Lavelle's unpaid bill.

"Uh-excuse me. Sister Lavelle Farrakhan...have you forgotten something?" Merrill waved the check like a warring nation's flag.

With a smile, Lavelle yelled as he walked out the door. "Sister cousin, thanks for getting this one. Call me. I love you." And with a wave of his slim fingers, Lavelle fluttered down Market Street. Tootle-loo!

"Triflin' ho!" Merrill muttered.

From behind him a low voice responded. "I hope you're not talking about me."

Merrill quickly turned and saw what Mariah Carey would call a vision of love. A dark-haired man with a broad, strong face smiled at him. Merrill was able to make out the streamlined curves of his finely defined shoulders and the thick cleave of his chest beneath the thick turtleneck sweater. His eyes settled on the sizable lump that rested thickly across the man's left leg. He wore yellow-gold hiking boots that perfectly matched his cream sweater. He looked up again and saw nothing but rows of perfect teeth. Merrill was taken aback when this gorgeous man placed a quick, soft kiss on his cheek.

"Sam's the name. Sam Chang. I sure hope to God you're Devon."

"Yeah, no. Actually, my real name's Merrill and Devon's my Internet handle." Merrill was seized with the sudden urge to kick himself. If Lavelle had taught him anything at all, it was that he was never to divulge his real name until he knew for sure he liked the guy. Sam pulled up a seat and threw his jacket over the back. Oh, he liked this guy alright, Merrill thought. Yup, things are gonna change around here.

3.

The phone woke Merrill; he was sure that it was Sam.

"Merrill!" a familiar voice called thinly from the bottom of Merrill's fuzzy consciousness.

"Merrill!" The voice called again.

"Lavelle?" Like he'd been hit with a splash of cold water, Merrill sat up and steeled himself for the confrontation ahead. He knew he had some explaining to do.

"Yes, Lavelle. Bitch, do you know what I had to go through to get your fucking phone number? What's up with the disappearing act? I called your job and they said it'd been almost six months since you left and *that* was six months ago! Are you getting yo' ass kicked again?"

"No, Lavelle, I'm not. It's just..."

"It's just *what*, Merrill? What have you gotten yourself into now?"

Sternly, Merrill responded. "It's not going down like what you think, OK? Just chill the fuck out!"

"Chill the fuck out? Oh, so you grown now? Tell me Ms. Merrill, you playing the happy housewife for Bruce Lee? What's up-and why haven't you called me? All I know is that I left town, and when I got back, you'd moved out of your place, quit your job. Poof! Just like that!"

"We got married." Merrill twisted the platinum ring that hung from the chain Sam brought him when he outgrew his ring fifty pounds ago.

"Married? Uh-uh Merrill, this shit sounds weird. Married? What do you mean married?"

"Married as in we committed to each other for life, OK? He don't hit me. He's the best man I've ever been with. He loves me."

"Alright, but you couldn't call me?"

"Just been busy 'Velle. Time flies, you know."

"No, I don't know"

"Besides, we just keep to ourselves. Sam's real private."

"Uh-huh, I see where this is going. You know what, it sounds like the same old shit to me so married or not I'm not pulling you out of the fire again, Merrill. I wish you and your husband a happy fucking marriage. But I'll just bet I'm gonna get a call when he kicks yo' ass to the curb."

Click. Merrill could feel the hurt in his cousin's voice. Hot tears started to roll down his boulder-like cheeks. He reached over for a tissue and his fruit punch. "It's not like that," Merrill muttered to the empty loft. "It's not like that. Sammy loves me. He's the only one who loves me." Merrill threw his head back and let the sweet syrupy punch wash the sadness and fear into the earthshaking grumbling of his waking stomach. Snack time.

4.

Merrill let Sam fuck him the very first time they made love. Merrill couldn't remember ever wanting to feel somebody inside him as much as he wanted Sam. Sam played him like a jazz musician, smooth and mellow. From their first date, Sam made it clear that he wanted to spend every day with Merrill, but Sam held off for at least three weeks before he allowed himself to indulge physically. He wanted to prove to Merrill and himself that he had serious intentions.

Every day was filled with gifts for Merrill. The first gift was a compilation tape that Sam put together. Sam told Merrill that the tape was a soundtrack to their romance, filled with songs he wanted to hear when they made love for the very first time. Sam's selections varied from Dinah Washington to the Fugees, from David Bowie to Thelonious Monk. It was clear to Merrill that he was being quickly swept off his feet; he had never dreamed that falling in love could be like this. His favorite songs on the cassette were the first song on the A-side which was The Fugees's version of "Killing Me Softly," and the very last song, which was "Wild Is the Wind" by David Bowie. Merrill listened to the tape every day and it didn't take him long to forget what life was like before Sam Chang.

Being that it was San Francisco, Merrill couldn't understand the strange reception he and Sam got when they walked down Castro. Asian men and black men looked at the pair strangely and it was obvious that they were trying hard to understand the nature of the relationship. White men ignored the fact that they were actually lovers and proceeded to hit on Sam or Merrill, depending on their fetish. Actually, it bothered Merrill more than Sam. For the most part, Sam found gay society to be too self-loathing to be supportive of relationships, much less interracial relationships. It wasn't hard for Merrill to see the truth in what Sam was saying, given his past relationships and the flighty nature of his friends. Sam preferred to be alone with Merrill, but he occasionally gave in to Merrill's need to show him off.

Sam had never met anyone who needed to be loved as much as Merrill. Merrill was Sam's dream come true. All his life, he had dreamed of someone who needed his love, someone totally dependent on his affections. He had tried a few times with other men but he found that they lacked the trust that was necessary to make themselves truly vulnerable to him. Sam was conscious of the lure his looks and his money presented but he sensed that Merrill's need to be loved went deeper than the crude desire for wealth or status. Sam especially loved Merrill for his shortcomings. Although he found Merrill to be exceptionally attractive, it was clear that Merrill didn't have the same sense of his own worth. Merrill, uncomfortable with his size, hid under baggy sweaters and loose slacks. He mistook the natural bigness of his body for obesity.

Merrill's size and his potential to grow greatly appealed to Sam. Unlike most gay men, Sam was not fixated on washboard stomachs and iron pecs in his lovers, although he was fairly obsessed with his own fitness regimen. Merrill's largeness of being increased the sexual potential for Sam. His best fantasies involved being smothered under layers and mounds of pillowy, warm flesh. He imagined Merrill's arms wrapping around him like a humid summer night until he was completely enveloped in his lover's need and gratitude. Deep in the folds of skin, he became one with his lover and he no longer felt alone. He reveled in the silky softness of flesh, so foolishly disregarded by other gay men who preferred the lean and taut-traits of the cruel and the miserly. What he needed most in a man was tenderness, a vulnerability that is rare in a society obsessed with vanity and independence.

When Sam first met Merrill he knew that there was some work to do before he could actualize his dream. Merrill was way too small. At six foot two, Merrill couldn't have been any more than two hundred and forty pounds and Sam had plans to put some meat on his lover's bones. Merrill's hunger to be loved made the possibility of Sam's plan more achievable, and he agreed to quit his job and move into Sam's waterfront loft. At first, it was under the pretense that Merrill would stay home both to be a good spouse to Sam and to pursue a music career. Three months and sixty pounds later, it was evident that there was to be no music career, just endless days of sleep, food, and undying love from Sam. Merrill felt like a fat, happy, cat: loved, fed, and content with his master.

5.

On Merrill's thirtieth birthday, Sam planned a celebration feast that took days to prepare. In addition to celebrating his birthday, Sam also wanted to celebrate his own achievement in bringing Merrill to the halfway point. At six hundred and fifty pounds, Merrill no longer needed clothes, at least that's what Sam determined. Sam made sure that the loft was sufficiently heated so that his lover never needed the warmth and protection that clothes provided. Having moved his office to the loft,

Sam was able to spend every day with Merrill, and the bliss and joy that it brought him were immeasurable.

Sustaining Merrill's weight required Sam's undivided attention. When Merrill needed to use the bathroom, it took almost fifteen minutes for him to get up from the mattress and make his way to the john. Sam replaced the standard porcelain bowl with a stronger industrial steel version to accommodate his weight. Sam made some other purchases, including a special hanging scale that could measure up to eight hundred pounds, enabling him to check on the progress of his endeavors. In order to keep Merrill's health at an optimum, Sam bought kits for measuring his lover's blood pressure and blood sugar level. Through the Internet, he was able to find the necessary health information, and sources for insulin and hypertension medication that decreased the likelihood of strokes or complications brought on by diabetes. Daily, he helped his lover walk the length of the apartment in order to keep his blood circulating and his body limber for the marathon lovemaking sessions that Sam initiated.

Sam hid and found treasures inside the thick folds of Merrill's expanding trunk. Oftentimes, he felt like an explorer or an archaeologist digging through civilizations of unexplored flesh. His hands often disappeared between the billowy folds of Merrill's belly and his pubic area. The sensation was similar to sinking his fists into a bowl full of warm hamburger. It was in this position that Sam would take Merrill in his mouth until his throat was filled with the thick, phlegmy sprays of his lover's cum. Merrill's strong perfume permeated the loft and for Sam it was an intoxicating aphrodisiac. Layers of sweat and dust formed black lines along the rims of fat that emphasized the shapes and folds of flesh that waved and jiggled with the slightest movement. Sam thought that Merrill was becoming more beautiful, resembling a slow-moving formation of hardening lava.

After what seemed to be hours of torturous anticipation, Sam finally came out of the kitchen with carts of food for the feast. Seven different restaurants began their deliveries and two bakeries prepared pies, a flan, and a cake big enough for a small wedding party. Lovingly, Sam arranged the heaping trays of food around Merrill. Around the bed, he fixed streamers and colorful birthday banners and lit a circle of candles that framed the perimeter of his lover's feast. Merrill's eyes twinkled with anticipation.

The pièce de résistance was the cake. Sam, now fully undressed, carried the three-layered cake and delicately placed it at his lover's feet. His cock was already tumescent and dripping a thick syrupy river of precum across his right thigh.

Merrill was breathless. The cake was beautiful: all roses and chocolate leaves. "Oh, Sam you shouldn't have!"

"This is the least I could do. Happy birthday, baby!"

A smooth script of red icing simply expressed the joy of this occasion: *Happy 30th Merrill! With undying love, Sam.*

All in a Day's Work

Quang H. Dang

A couple of years back, I figured out I could catch the attention of a guy I'm cruising in the woods by snapping small twigs, following behind him. *Tip #1: Don't be afraid to experiment with different techniques. Rustling leaves is good too—unparalleled in dramatic effect, but loses points for sheer biomechanical inefficiency.*

Today, things were not looking so promising. There I was, shin-high in a nest of odd branches and ends, and this fine Filipino brother had not once glanced over his sturdy shoulders my way. He wasn't more than twenty-four, his shorts were very Oscar de la Hoya, and in my favorite baby blue-so pale it seems impossible they're still blue. And thighs so thick they stretched and gathered the baggy material that hung on his hips.

A light dusting of dark hairs ran down my Filipino Oscar's tightly drawn calves to his fresh socks. *Tip #2: When they've got black sneakers on-and my Oscar was wearing original-issue soccer-type sambas-you go to the whiteness of the socks if you want to know how long they've been cruising the woods.* He must have just gotten there. As long as I was looking down at his feet, I studied for any other giveaway signs: no nervous shuffle, not a single come-here toe tap.

His T-shirt was inside-out and charcoal gray, so worn the brown of his shoulder blades glowed through the seams. The soft fabric hugging his thick waist anchored onto his expanding back. Again, those sturdy shoulders, superhuman hinges opening into his meaty arms.

Pivoting a few steps, I could now make out his face. The expression was cool, but unmistakably sensual. The sort of man who could stare right through you with just the slightest wrinkle between his dark eyes. Make your ears burn when your gaze drops to your feet. And when your eyes can't help but go back to his, he'd smooth that wrinkle out, hinting just enough of a smile for you to say your body was all his.

His nose was broad and flat, like mine, and his plump, plum-brown lips propped up a neat mustache. I imagined the first kiss: the hairs would be too soft to tickle really, but I wondered if he would push his tongue into my mouth, or draw mine into his? Would he prefer pressing our full lips together, or is he the biting type? Now, my chest sat tight on my heavy stomach, and my mouth was so dry my lips wouldn't move, even if I had a thing to say. *Tip #3: Breathe.*

He started walking away. Previously, his round ass had been concealed by his gray, untucked shirt, but now it was lifting proudly as he walked. I knew I was not going to get a piece of my Oscar today, but I was still curious to see what he was going to go after. *Tip #4: Don't set your heart on a man who is clearly not interested. Hopelessly pining after unattainable cuties is best left for every-day life, not park cruising. Tip #5: Besides, if you play it cool enough, you can still catch him plopping it out for someone else, so stay tuned.*

What's this now though? My Oscar walked his proud ass right past this beautiful Latino man. I could have sworn they paused an extra second and threw each other nods. Oh, the thought of catching those two getting it on. Imagine how my heart sank when my Oscar kept on walking and settled for a severely nondescript man. You know, the type of white man who was not dressing, walking, or aging gracefully. He apparently had no qualm about wearing white—and I mean really white—running shoes with very pressed, very tapered slacks. My Filipino Oscar de La Hoya had passed me and the Latino beauty up for Jerry Seinfeld meets Cousin Balki from television's "Perfect Strangers."

I continued on my way, feeling like leaving the park altogether. Stubborn by nature though, and horny by the way, I decided this was no time to leave. *Tip #6: Pick yourself up, dust yourself off...* There were plenty of other sections of this park to be scanned.

It got real quiet once I crossed onto a grassy meadow from the grainy dirt patch where my Oscar was last seen. It wasn't long before footsteps fell in behind me, muffled by the grass.

I wasn't quite cool enough to glance back and see what he looked like. But I had honed my technique in some of the darkest pitches of nighttime cruising. *Tip #7: Like Steffi Graf with her forehand, build your game around your strengths.* My trusty hearing would have to serve me now. I rounded back onto another dusty path. Behind me: crunch crunch, crunch, crunch....

I slowed down a quarter-step, as I headed up a small hill. Behind me, the crunching steps mimicked my syncopated climbing, accompanied by quickened breath, and punctuated with the metallic swish of a running suit. *Tip #8: Beware: Running suits are notoriously misleading, as far as indicators go. You may end up in casual/active wear Hunksville, or you could just be destined for a shiny, tacky dresser.* Hmmm, now if my memory was serving me correctly, that Latino man my Oscar had passed up was wearing running suit pants. *Tip #9: Keep your mind sharp by playing games like Memory in your spare time. Group games are a good way of keeping in touch with your friends anyway.*

The hill leveled out, and I found myself in front of a view breathtaking enough to justify pausing. The swishing neared, and tstarted past; like an ambulance siren, the running pants zipped loudest and fastest directly behind me. I turned; I was right. The source of my fading Doppler effect was the Latino guy Oscar had passed up.

Before I could think of anything to say, he came back over and with a slight curl of his lip, said, "Eh, Kumusta."

"I'm not Filipino," I answered, adding, "but I'm doing just fine."

His brown skin blushed a half-shade, and he apologized, explaining that his lover was Filipino, and he's so familiar with the relatives that it's almost automatic for him now to greet, well, "Ehh, certain Asians, who look, ehhhrrr, darker, or you know, less..."

I had to stop him there, "It really is okay. It's nice to meet you." *Tip #10: Talking is not required, and should often be discouraged.*

He proceeded to ask me the two questions I can't stand. How are you supposed to answer, "What are you up to?" and "What do you like to do?" I managed to bobble through something about being out for a walk, but I took a slight hop on the landing. *Tip #11: Everybody knows "What do you like to do?" is really, "Do you like to fuck? Top or bottom?" If you can pull it off, try something coy like, "We're going to have to find that out together, don't you think?"* Today, all I could naively offer was, "Oh, I like to hang out with friends, go for drinks, just mellow stuff." *Tip #12: Don't say you like to play Memory.*

That seemed to do the trick, but then he started telling me about himself, even asked me my name after introducing himself as Pedro. I wasn't feeling apple pie enough to be Mike, but not quite ethnic enough to be Tran. I'd already said I wasn't Filipino, so Archibald was out. So I settled on "Eddie," short for the very authentic, pan-Asian-American name Edwin. *Tip #13: Don't hesitate to give out a fake name. There's an assumption of risk that everyone takes when cruising the woods. On the rare occasion that you actually get to know the guy later, and the subject of your fake name comes up, you can laugh it off. Or if you have an especially Asian-sounding name, you can always just tell him that your trick name is your American name.*

"You have somewhere we can go, Eddie?" *Tip #14: Think Fast.*

Well, let's see, Eddie would be the sort of guy who's studying accounting at State, and lives at home with Ma and Grandma, so, "No, I live with my folks. How about you?"

"Yeah, I just dropped my boyfriend off at work so we got my place for a couple hours." *Tip #15: There is a lot of information to be gleaned from introductory pleasantries. Pedro is telling me he is in a relationship, there is some form of fixed income in their household, and more basically, he's gay identified. Remember a lot of so-called straight guys do the parks.*

The drive over to Pedro's apartment took ten minutes tops, maybe another five to find parking. We talked the whole way. I felt like I was in a total porn movie or something. He kept asking me provocative questions about what sex I liked. *Tip*

#16: You never know when someone has gotten their hands on Making Safe Sex Hotter material.

Despite all this talking, Pedro was quite "dating fine." Tip #17: Generally, you may have to lower your usual standards for what you would date for guys you meet at the park. But you can still be choosy. Nothing is more frustrating than settling for someone less than ideal and then walking past LL Cool J on your way out of the bushes. His thick goatee was perfectly groomed, his slightly wavy hair lightly greased back, and when he talked he licked his lips every few words, leaving them fetchingly moist. Usually if I'm park cruising, I'd just as soon grab what I can in the bushes, but the thought of Pedro in bed was worth all this conversation.

His body was solid and compact, with a slight curve at his belly. Every move he made, even just sitting in the car driving, looked perfectly comfortable.

His place seemed small for both Pedro and a boyfriend to live in, but it was orderly and clean. He sat me on the futon at the end of the studio and offered me some water. On the way to the sink, he turned down a framed picture frame. *Tip #18: Never ask questions about your trick's boyfriend or girlfriend.*

"Is that your boyfriend?" *Tip #19: I guess Tip #18 is optional They're all just guidelines anyway. It's not rocket science.*

"Yeah, I still feel a little weird about bringing guys here, even though we have an agreement. It'd be fine if he were here, but I feel guilty having all this fun while he's out there working."

"What's your agreement?" He explained: They've been together four years and love each other very much, have always had an open relationship—but it's been hard since they started living together.

"This studio is so small, but we need to save money. I'm sick of working retail for other people, and Leo hates what he has to put up with for his job, so we really want to open up our own business, maybe a café. Neither one of us has ever lived with anyone before. We agreed to have our trade sex in other places whenever we can. It's fine here as long as it doesn't become a regular thing." *Tip #20: The sweet ones always love to talk, talk, talk. If you find yourself going crazy, crazy, crazy, take matters firmly in hand.*

I blurted out, "Do you want to fuck me?"

"What? No kissing and cuddling first?" he joked.

"Sure, that's all good, I just want to get cleaned up before we get into it." *Tip #21: When talking about anal hygiene, use vague, nondescriptive terms.* Pedro showed me the bathroom. Inside, I checked the mirror: I was beaming.

The front door of the apartment slammed, then a voice, half shouting, half laughing, "Fucking crazy cheap ass cracker, wouldn't give me more than a fifty. He just wanted to suck my toes though. Whatever. At least this pays the phone bill."

"I got someone here," Pedro interrupted, and then all I could hear were whispers.

Pedro knocked at the door and I let him in, but he didn't say anything, so I tried to catch his eye. "I guess that's that, huh? Is he mad?"

"No, ehhr, Leo wants all three of us to have a little fun."

"What? He doesn't even know what I look like."

"Actually, he likes very much what you look like."

Before I could consider much what Pedro meant, Leo called in, "C'mon you guys, can you process out here? I want to get these clothes off and wash, especially my toes."

The door creaked open, and a dark hand pitched toward the hamper under the sink a charcoal-gray T-shirt, two not-so-white-anymore socks, and a pair of impossibly baby blue shorts.

So This Is What Girls Do?

S'Naughty Spice

The tourists are back in San Francisco for the onslaught of parades and street fairs, underdressed for the summer fog, and shivering as they stroll through the Castro. But this year June has been surprisingly hot, routinely in the eighties, with even a touch of humidity. I am getting home later and later. My house-mate Hermin-Mino we call him-is dragging his butt in the door at around the same time, early in the morning. Each night we make the rounds of bars, dance clubs, and sex clubs talking to people about HIV; he talks to men and I talk to women.

"Hi honey," I mumble from the sofa where I am sprawled, still in my club clothes.

"Hey," Mino mumbles back with the same note of exhaustion in his voice. He grabs some lemonade out of the icebox and pours two glasses.

"How was your night?" I call.

"OK. I was at Steamworks. Same ol' same ol'. Talk, flirt, hand out condoms...talk, flirt, hand out condoms, turn down propo-sition, talk some more...and yours?" Mino hands me a glass and collapses into a chair nearby.

"I saw the Safer Sex Sluts do a demo at the club I was at tonight. Girrrrl, they were hot," I say, perking up a bit.

"Yeah? What did they do-line up like two-steppers and—" He makes feeble two-fingered jabs forward as if he is finger-fucking someone.

"Fuck you! Is that all you can come up with for women to do together? There are a couple of other things we've figured out since the beginning of time. When did you last have sex with a woman anyway? At fourteen? Fifteen? Maybe sixteen?"

"Fifteen, I was fifteen," he sighs, knowing what comes next.

"Oh...I see...and I am so sure you knew exactly how to make a woman cum when you were fifteen." I am crabby, hot, and quickly getting louder. "You probably couldn't tell the difference between her cunt and her asshole, much less have had even the vaguest idea where her clit or G-spot were, or how long to fuck her in any one position, or how hard or how soft..."

"OK. OK," Mino says, managing to break into my impromptu diatribe. "I get the point. I'm sorry. So...what were they doing?"

I am not satisfied with his apology, mutter something incoherent about motorcycles and cherries, and continue. "You know, I am so sick of this shit! Everyone has some bullshit to lay on me. I get crap from lesbians I date who are scared I'm gonna run off with a man. And tonight at work, this one bitch sat there, right after telling me she fucked a man the month before without a condom, and told me she did not have to practice safer sex with lesbians because lesbians don't have AIDS—it's just those damn bisexual women that are spreading that shit around. Who the fuck does she think she is? As if?!"

I am yelling now, and talking as fast as I can, "And then straight men who are paranoid about every female friend I have, convinced I'm cheating on them. And the bisexuals I meet are so caught up in their identity crap that they forget how to have sex or look good or, fuck it, even wash themselves. A clean head of hair will go a long way in the 'bisexual community.'

Community, my ass. I hate that word. Every single community I know of is defined not by who is in it but by the people they keep out. I am not part of any community. I am sick of community. I am queer, I am brown, and I will fuck whoever I want whenever I want and I will take my lover wherever I want and anyone who doesn't like it can just fuck the fuck off!"

"Whooooa! Whooooa, dude. Slow down. Easy there!" He is attempting to be soothing but he is laughing too hard. "What can of worms did I just open?"

I am not smiling. "The stupid AIDS Office and Department of Public Health decided not to continue funding our program because for some reason they don't believe that queer women of color are at risk."

"Damn," he says, concerned, "What's Rafael planning to do?"

"He's looking for additional funding, but as of now, I'm out of a job come September. They extended our contract a couple months so there won't be any 'gaps in service.' So the stupid gaps will appear a few months later. Whatever. I hate them."

Mino and I have been friends for ten years and housemates for five. We have seen each other through so much: relationships and breakups, evil parental visits, happy reunions with siblings, his positive HIV test result, and, just three years ago next month, my best friend/sometime girlfriend's death from AIDS and my subsequent negative HIV test results. I am not a person who opens up to very many people, and since Alayna's passing, he has been my primary support, friend, and shoulder to cry on.

He comes over and puts his arms around me. We are both sweating so we just sit there, sticking to the couch and to each other. Trying to change the subject, I ask him, "So, have you ever thought about fucking a woman? Since you were fifteen, that is."

There is a long pause. I cannot stand the silence, so I urge him, "Be honest."

It is Mino's turn to change the subject. He gets up and walks back to the icebox. "I love Mitchell's. They make ice cream like no one else can even imagine it. You want mango? I'm having ube."

I nod. Waiting.

"Well..." he does his imitation of Samantha from "Bewitched." "I can say that I have, on occasion, well, every once in a while, when I'm not...Do I have to answer this?"

I am enjoying his discomfort. "Yes."

"Well then, maybe," he states matter-of-factly.

"Details."

"No."

"Why not?"

"Because."

"Because why?"

"Because!"

I giggle. I know he hates when I giggle because I only do that when I have a plan. And my plans rarely benefit him. Accordingly, Mino gives me a suspicious look.

"What? Stop giggling!" Now I am just smiling. "I hate it when you do that! What?"

"Would you fuck me?" I ask mischievously.

"NO!!" He yells louder than he had planned.

I giggle again. "Come on," I tease, "I'll strap it on for you like I did for Chino. He liked it. And he's fucked boys. He has something to compare it to."

"No," he sulks, and takes his ice cream into the bathroom. I giggle one last time as he gently shuts the door. A few seconds later, I hear the shower turn on.

As I begin to eat my ice cream, the first gay porn I ever watched pops unexpectedly into my head. The opening shot is of a man, hands bound, blindfolded, laid out on his side on a bench, maybe six men around him in varying states of undress and weird faux military uniforms. And a guy watching from afar in a smoking jacket. The guy on the bench has a dick in his mouth and another in his ass, one guy sucking his cock, and the rest jerking off while standing over him. They all take turns with the guy on the bench, who looks like he is trying really hard to pretend he does not like this.

I can feel my heart rate increase slightly. Even the cheesiest stuff makes me hot. The smoking jacket man lights a pipe. There is a lovely view of the hills in L.A. Then a similar series of shots repeated over and over, dicks in mouths, in butts, moving, thrusting, hands faster and faster until miraculously, all of them cum, all at the same time, all over the guy on the bench.

As always, I close my eyes for that last moment. I hate watching men ejaculate. For me it is nothing more than a messy sneeze that tastes and smells like uncooked yeast. It's not that I don't like men or their bodies. I love having sex with men, I like the way their bodies feel and smell and taste. And I have wanted to top a gay man since I realized they exist. I'm not sure where this weird ejaculation thing comes from.

I know it is not a fear of sexuality or fluids or viscera, because women are a different story, pungent and sweet, I can drink their juices up all night. Of course, one might wonder how I know what such things taste like in this day and age of latex and Saran wrap. I guess we all choose our risks.

I move into my bedroom and finish about half of my ice cream, savoring each bite, when suddenly he is in the room with me, wearing his minuscule navy blue towel. His hair is wet and sticking up all over the place and there are a few drops of water remaining on the back of his neck. I think about licking them off.

He plops on my bed like a sack of potatoes and remains there, motionless, staring at the ceiling. "Are you scared?" I ask gently.

"No," he responds, "It's just...well...it's just...weird."

"That was descriptive," I retort. "Because of our friendship?"

"No. Well, you're different from most people I know. Hell, you're soooo bisexual its disgusting."

"I am NOT bisexual," I interrupt.

"OK, but, well, you'll fuck..."

"...Anything that moves," I finish for him in a snotty tone.

"No, but gender, male, female, trans, race, color, whatever, don't seem to affect your choices much. Except," he draws out his words, "longhaired Koreans do seem to make regular appearances...."

"Enough!" I interrupt, again.

"Anyway," he continues, "how many women do you know, straight or queer, that would fuck an HIV+ gay man? It's hard enough finding a man, and at least I have my pickup act together for them. But the inevitable discussions about disclosure and so on-what would I say?"

"Women have heard of HIV, but I get your point," I concede.

Then we turn, out of habit, to our usual sex discussions. But tonight there is a new twist, we're talking about girls.

"So do you like women's bodies? Do they turn you on?"

"I feel a twinge sometimes when I watch the Spice channel, does that count?"

I look at him with disgust. "Funny."

"I haven't really thought about having sex with a woman for years. Living in San Francisco you can just forget that women exist as erotic objects," he notices the fire in my eyes and stutters, "almost...I mean...you know what I mean."

"Not really," I snap.

"It's just not something I think about every day."

"Me neither."

"Would you stop with the one-liners?!" he pleads.

"Do you like pussy?" I ask, finally getting to the point.

"Eeewwwehh! Escargot...snail trails 'n things."

"Misogynist! They are not snail trails and I hate snails," I reply petulantly. "Do you like eating pussy?"

"Definitely NO," he says, squealing with mock fright. "I'm not going there again."

I am rolling my eyes and laughing now. "What about titties?"

"Eeeeeeeeh." He makes his patented old man noise and then slowly replies, "I like playing with 'em on men...it's just...women don't do anything for me. Not a damn thing. I don't know why."

An endless moment of silence follows. I have fucked a lot of men, all shapes, sizes, and colors, trans and not, but never a gay man. It's hard to convince a gay man to fuck you when you're a woman. But I've always wanted to. For all their stereotyped promiscuity, gay men are harder to seduce than straight girls. And I want them more because of it. There is something so erotic about the unattainable. All my hottest masturbation fantasies are about gay men; well, me as a dirty old man too, but that's another story.

I turn my head to look at him and notice how good Mino is looking right now, and remember how long it's been since I've had sex. Nothing makes three months drag like a lack of sex. I reach for the edge of his towel and pull it open. He continues to lie there.

All I can think is that he is a little skinnier than I usually like in a boy. I like enough flesh to grab on to and dig in. And I like to watch the marks of my crooked front teeth appear, reddening a circle around otherwise flawless chocolate skin so like my own.

But he will do nicely.

Inspired, I reach for a scrap of silk which serves as a blindfold. At first he tries to push my hands away, but I brush him aside and knot the scarf. His hands, suddenly a nuisance, I bind quickly with a belt I find lying on the floor, lashing him to the bedpost. My intuition is right, for once he cannot see or touch me, he relaxes. I leave on enough clothes to disguise the parts of my body which would stress him out. The stretch vinyl barely covers my breasts and cunt and it is hot and sticky on this moist summer evening.

My lips and hands slowly examine every bit of his neck and back, the metallic salt of a long summer day filling my mouth with bitterness even after his quick rinse in the shower. I scrape my teeth and tongue down his spine to his asshole, spreading him. He willingly submits and I bury my face between his cheeks. The exquisite smell of rotting flowers overpowers me and I taste him. I can feel his body shudder as goosebumps rise on his back, ignoring the wet heat of the night. But I do not linger, and move down his legs to his feet, lapping at the vinegar between his toes. On my way back up, I rest my cheek against him in the softest of skin between his hip bones on his lower belly. We are both surprised to find him rock hard. Smelling yeast between his legs, I trace a line with my tongue from his asshole over his balls to the base of his cock, exploring every fold.

His dick is slender but stubborn. And beautiful in its own mysterious way. I pause and just look up at him for a few moments: his strong yet graceful hands bound to the bedpost, his body firm, dark, and smooth.

His skin is cool to the touch. On his face, a look of confusion mixed with desire. I like that look.

Time to pull on my silicon. I smile as I think of all the conversations we have had about my dildos. Men always think women wear dildos because of that Freudian lack thing. Personally the only reason I would want a penis is so that when I am backpacking I don't have to take off my backpack and drop my pants to piss, offering prime meat for mosquitoes. I love dildos because you pick the size, as big or small as you want. They are always willing and never get tired or raw. And, when was the last time you heard of a guy who could keep from ejaculating for an hour and a half for his multi orgasmic girlfriend? If you find him, please give him my number.

I slip on a condom out of habit and feel a sudden rush of pleasure at having had the foresight to finally invest in a decent strap. It really makes all the difference. For tonight I choose my biggest, blackest, loveliest geometric dildo. A series of concentric triangles. It's big and rough and makes me feel the same way. Perfect to initiate my favorite boy.

I push his face and shoulders to the mattress while I spread his legs, presenting him quite attractively. Smearing on some lube, I contemplate his ass, deciding how to begin. I slide my finger, slick and wet, down the base of his spine to his asshole.

I let my finger rest there, touching that sweet pucker of skin. He is silent, barely breathing, and tense with anticipation. I slowly increase the pressure on my finger and ease it in. He tries to push back against me to force my finger deeper, but I can easily hold him down from this angle, and keep my movements gentle. I tease him with my slender fingers and he shivers with impatience, wanting more, but not daring to admit it.

When I feel he has waited long enough, I enter him. As I slide my fat fourteen-inch dildo into his ass, Mino sucks in his breath with a wet noise. I pause for a moment to let him adjust because today, I am very, very big. Slowly, I begin to move, grabbing his hips. As I begin to thrust a little faster, I hear his breath quicken and I can feel heat rising from deep within his body to the surface of his skin.

He tries to shift as I am grinding his knees into the bed, but I have the advantage and keep him in position. He is grunting as I begin to pound him really hard, with a fast, even rhythm. When I reach around to grab his balls tightly in my fist, he gives a deep guttural moan, one that surprises me. Even with the paper-thin walls of our two-bedroom flat, I have never heard him make this particular sound. It excites me, so I work a little harder, leaning into him with my full weight, slamming him.

My clit is rubbing against the strap and I am sopping wet. After working for a while, my groans begin to mingle with his, and I feel him cum all over himself, his chest and face. Then, I rock with my own orgasm, pushing deeper and deeper into him, clutching his ass and straining my nipples against the vinyl now slick with sweat. My orgasms are long and violent and I make him wait until I am done. He is panting, we are both dripping with sweat. I collapse onto the cool sheets next to him and untie his wrists. The leftovers of my orgasm make my abdomen buzz as my wet skin melts into the vinyl. He slides the blindfold off and rolls over. After he mops the thinning cum from his face and chest, he props himself up on one elbow, raises an eyebrow, and asks,

"So this is what girls do?"

I just smile knowingly and reach for the mango ice cream, but it has all melted. Sigh.

King Rubber

Lawrence Chua

You're sitting on a rock in the sea with your cousin Ah Meng, casting for small silvery fish that lose themselves in the reflecting sun. Trying to retrieve a tangled line, you slice open your leg and now it's bleeding in the heat. You both ignore the red syrup trickling like embarrassment around your feet. It's so red it looks fake. Ah Meng catches small flat pomfret, one after the other. The bucket is filled with them. Later, the small bones of the fish will pierce your tongue as your teeth try to separate the flesh. The only fish you manage to catch is a small fat tiger fish. You feel like a real star, barely suppressing your confidence. Your cousin is excited and congratulates you as you try to dislodge the hook from its throat.

Back on the beach, sliding frozen shrimp over your hooks. A hotel casts its shadow on your back as you wade into the water and swing your lines as far as the tide will allow. The bait keeps disintegrating off your hook. Ah Meng is your height and not very handsome. Uncle doesn't know what to do with him. He's been out of school for a few months now, and he spends his days fishing. Occasionally, he'll help your uncle doing construction work, but it's never for more than a few hours at a time. Ba would have beat a better work ethic into him. Ba. His brother. Your uncles. Your birth certificate classifies them as khek. It means they are the children of mercenaries and pirates. Passengers in every nation. People who settle when they run out of prospects.

Ah Meng is far down the shore and you're fixing a new line. A man wanders over from the part of the beach reserved for hotel guests. He has dark-blonde hair sticking out of a baseball cap, a mustache, a wide, softening chest with dollar-sized nipples, and a full, hard stomach rounded over bikini briefs. Even from this distance you can tell his hair is a toupee, but still he has a certain pig-bottom charm. When he talks in English with a severe Danish halt, you smile back.

-What is it?

He asks slowly, loudly, pointing to the melting shrimp in your hand.

-*Udang.*

You play along, fumbling for the English word. He guesses it before you say it. Then, without pause or segue, he asks you to rub suntan lotion on his back. Your cousin seems closer than he was before. The man's flesh looks as pink as the rotting thing in your hand. He's waiting for your answer.

You walk through the lobby of his hotel without a single thought in your mind. No one challenges you as you take the elevator up to his suite. He opens the door and ushers you inside without a word. The air-conditioning is on full blast. You can feel it pricking your skin, but when he runs his hands over you he says you're hotter than a firecracker. He's dressed in his bikini and a short-sleeved cotton shirt. He asks you to sit on the bed patiently. He takes off his clothes, fishes around in his suitcase, and comes up with a flat piece of black rubber. You wonder what it is, but before you can ask he slips it over his enormous ass. A pair of black rubber shorts that threaten to smother his erection.

He smiles at you. You smile back and slip two of your fingers down the front of the shorts, pull them out, and let them snap-back. He whimpers. You grope for multiple meanings behind his expression, but only one simple translation is possible.

He produces another piece of rubber. A shirt. And then another, that unfolds into a half mask, leaving his eyes staring out from an impenetrable flatness. There is a hardness missing from the rubber's surface. A lack that makes him look, somehow, more intelligent. Somehow, more inviting. But his new skin is too matte to the touch. It drags, tears at your flesh, and threatens to burn. You need to get it wet. You pull the shorts out again. Stick your limp penis down the front and breathe. Try to relax your body. When that doesn't work, you try to make your body disappear. Your flesh falls away, recedes into a red lacquer box, scarred by smooth drips running horizontally across its glazed sides. You watch the hinges close on you and calm your breath. On the fifth expulsion of air, you feel it start to trickle out and then stop. You start again, and this time a torrent of urine pushes out. He is surprised, but it only takes a moment before it fades into indignation. You put your hand over his mouth and continue urinating. You are surprised at how quickly your bladder fills his shorts. It starts dribbling out the legs of his shorts, coursing down his hairy calves. His eyes close. His breath stains your fingers, rude against your skin. You push him down, still peeing. Cover him with your body. The rubber takes on a new sheen. You feel his bones twisting underneath the thin membranes separating you. He turns on his side, so the two of you are facing each other. Run your hands over his chest, pulling at the elastic, clutching at the flesh beneath. You fall against him as if he were solid pavement, realizing too late that his body is not about armored plating but smooth clouds of slaughter. The meat hangs off the bone only slightly out of shape. Tired. A belly. A black stream crossing that belly covers you, implicates you in this little elastic web of violence. This was muscle once, you think, as surely as the cash-crop plantations around you were once a forest.

You insert a finger past his sphincter. It closes warm and wet around the first digit, and you dial it as if it were a telephone. But when you connect, it occurs to you that you do not know for whom to ask. You do not know his name. You open your mouth to ask, but the words get stuffed in your lungs. You bring your teeth against his chest, breathing deeply. Sweat. Piss. Latex. Deodorant. Swallow the whole earth. Drink the whole sea. He whimpers underneath you as your jaw grinds his two membranes against each other.

There is a pimple at the base of flesh separating his legs and he winces every time you brush it. You have learned to call this part of anatomy *taint.* Some queen somewhere lodged it in your vocabulary: *'Tain't ass and 'tain't dick.* But perhaps there is also the suggestion of spoilage and poison here. Following the discovery of the economic importance of rubber at the beginning of the century, South American leaf blight *(Microcyclus ulei)* became a much-feared disease because of its devastating effect on the rubber-producing plant *Hevea brasiliensis.* The disease is most conspicuous on the leaves. Infection results in repeated defoliation, dieback of the canopy, and death, even of mature trees. As the leaf hardens, the lesions lose their powdery appearance and become brownish, and the center may rot away. It is possible that the spread could have happened through attempts to grow rubber outside the natural range of the genus. Through attempts to expand production.

You spread your hand greedily across the seamless expanse of his backside. You notice what you did not see before: broken blood vessels, like fine hairs or brush strokes, crossing his ass. Railway lines. Capillaries without origin or destination. The remnants of some archaic verse. Your hand rises and then bears down with the force of frustration. You hear it crack across the room, bringing the desired effect. Grab him by the hair, pull him down off the bed. Make him crawl around the floor, as you undress. He licks at your calves as you expose them, but the effect is unsatisfying. His humiliation is merely perfunctory. You feel the urge to make it sublime.

Under colonial capitalism, industriousness was symbolized by the mule. The Malay unwillingness to expend labor on the plantations led to the characterization of the local population as lazy. The indentured coolies from abroad, however, earned the reputation of being "mules among nations." The laborers imported by coolie brokers in South China, Hong Kong, and Singapore were also called "piglets," and the people in charge of their lodging houses were called "heads of piglets."

Your fingers pull at his flesh, lifting muscle, cartilage, and skin from the bone. Probing. Exorcising his body, because evil always produces itself in the flesh. The master narrative of the original sin perpetuates itself in every shudder and twitch of our muscles. The wages of sin have bought the foundation for the ideology of exploitation. An ideology that could be the answer to all your problems, but it's not. Disillusioned, your hands return the flesh to his body. You search elsewhere, shoving four fingers in his mouth, pulling on his jaw. But in the end, you are just too lazy to rip it off his face. A conflict stirs in your gut. A conflict of belief. The conflict, essentially, is whether to accumulate or subsist. Whether to own the flesh you are touching or simply to pass through and over it, leaving it intact and alive. You remember something vaguely, a rule of economic culture: A production system that is not mechanized does not build surplus.

A vibrator would be nice. You look around for something to keep him full. Something low-maintenance. A cucumber. A dildo. That would have required premeditation. Instead, you work with what is available. A long-necked bottle of beer from the minibar. A belt from his suitcase. A hand towel from the bathroom.

You truss him up like a pig. No. That's wrong. He looks more like a package. His knees bleed into his chest until he is just a lump of sweaty rubber and muscle, his face gurgling in the scratchy triangle of your crotch. You grab him by the hair. Tie a hand towel emblazoned with the hotel logo into a knot. Stuff the knot in his mouth and tie the ends around his head. Lower his face in tribute. Or in shame. You uncap the beer bottle and pour its contents all over him. It slaps across the burning sea of his back, erasing the drying white salt licks you left behind on the rubber. Through his pleasure, he exhales. It is a wounded breath you hear as you spread his ass apart with your hands and spit on his sphincter. There are a few encrusted hairs there. The crumbs seem almost unreal, as if they are too perfectly formed to have been produced organically. His body becomes a thing underneath you.

Take a step out. Not far. Just enough to feel yourself falling. Press the mouth of the empty bottle against his asshole. It puckers, trembles, and then locks around the stem. You are surprised at how smoothly it slides in. You marvel at how far it goes in. The bottle might break. That is the reality of things. Bend a thing back too far and it snaps. He shudders against the glass. You feel your hand against it but can't tell if it's you or the glass that's trembling. You're all sticky with sweat. It's two hours later. He's lying on his back, with his knees touching the sides of the bed by his head. Remove the bottle. Play more closely with his fleshy ass, alternating your tongue with three well-greased fingers. You feel heat that was only suggested through glass. Power suggested only by the position of your hand at the axis of his body. He's trying to get his own dick in his mouth. Your suggestion. The tip of his tongue can barely touch the head. He says he's close, but you know he doesn't mean it in terms of space. He spends it all over his face, with his mouth wide open in disbelief. It's splattered all over his cheeks, and you help him clean up by wiping it into his mouth. He sucks on your fingers for a while and then, finally, you let him kiss you.

You're in the shower. He's sleeping. It's getting dark outside. Everything has a strange kind of sadness in this afternoon light. The air conditioner is singing over your head. He's snoring. The only changes in the room are two fifty-ringgit notes underneath the lamp by the bed.

The Widow Season

Philip Huang

Paul and nights of fevers.

The horse I couldn't see. Paul would measure the animal's height with his hands. Eighteen hands, he'd tell me. He said it would nose the sores on his body like sugar cubes on an open palm and sometimes the whiskers would break the ballooning skin. And only once was he able to climb that matted mane and conquer and escape, his figure magnificent, astride. Horseman riding with the world in chase. Watch for me, he said.

August seventeenth.

That's what I was doing when he died, watching for that horse. But there was nothing. No horse. When the nurse finally came, the only movement in the room was that of Paul's fists slowly unraveling, the fingers gracefully unfolding, as if he were revealing a secret he'd held on to in his palms.

And I said to nobody in particular: It's over, Pooh. It just is.

***

I never liked this flat. The houses on the block were too close together, I thought, like impacted teeth. But Paul loved the idea of a long hallway that leads into a small back garden. Like a birth canal, or the path to a sacrificial altar, he said. A liminal space. I said he was a morbid bastard. He said I was projecting.

We moved in one morning six years ago. I followed the rented U-Haul in my car, watching Paul's studious face in the side-view mirror and his mother's limp cigaretted arm dangling out of the passenger-side window. Once we pulled up to the address, Paul's mother climbed down from the cab, her tiny body rigid beneath an oversized dress of something floral, and dragged from her cigarette as she squinted at the house. While Paul backed the truck into the driveway, I unlocked the door for Elizabeth and swept out an arm as a sign of goodwill: Tadah! She bent her head tentatively over the threshhold as if entering a cave and toured the rooms indifferently, occasionally kicking at a wall, her lips pursed, her pug face revealing neither mild dislike nor pleasure. Then she produced a gilded fan from her jacket and, without asking, hung it over the empty mantel: to blow out the ghosts, Paul later explained.

Looking through the front door where Paul was unloading boxes at the curb, she sighed, "Well, I suppose you boys are married now."

I nodded. It was one of the few times she ever spoke directly to me. Then she leaned in, the two gray stitches of her eyebrows rising, the short blunt of her hair sliding forward, and through her teeth she whispered sharply: "Don't screw this up." Her earrings were the size of foreign coins and they swung to and fro a half-beat behind her earlobes. As she leaned forward, her perfume wafted toward me and I thought of museum cellars filled with tattered scrolls.

Her family had been swept into an internment camp somewhere in the Arizona desert when she was a girl, and she gave us a photo of the camp orchestra to put on our tiny mantel. That is to say: she put the photo squarely on the mantel, then smiled at it a second as if the house had suddenly come into focus-a deliberate and public christening, thereby forbidding all future debates about its place in our home. This would be her house, too, she was saying. Columbus planting his Spanish flag on Indian soil. Or maybe it was a jab at my being Chinese and an immigrant, while she and her son were Japanese-Americans. Nisei history laid bare atop our hearth.

At Paul's funeral, Elizabeth stood across the open earth from me, her eyes glassed over in the preacher's direction. I followed her gaze to the sky just above a grove of tombstones in the distance.

I drove home with one hand resting on the passenger seat.

In the bedroom I undressed in the dark, then poured a glass of wine and stood drinking against the mantel, looking at the furniture in the living room. The long dimple on the sofa where Paul and I would lie for hours in the evening, his sleeping arms holding me; in front of the sofa, like a deformed pet sleeping in the half-light, the three-legged coffee table Paul had rescued from a neighbor's curb; on the walls, Paul's framed diplomas, the psychiatric license that proved, he would remind me, his clinical disinterest in calling me neurotic and passive-aggressive.

I rested the wine-glass on the mantel and something grazed my knuckles. Oh yes, the photograph Elizabeth had planted there. Over the years the mantel had come to harbor a jar of pennies and an endless rotation of ceramic or glass animals Paul would buy for pocket change and bring home. He used them in play therapy with some of his patients, and on me. Elizabeth's photo had been exiled to the edge of the mantel top. But the light from the street filtered through the wine-glass and focused to a point right at the center of the picture.

Like the giant Alice peering into the White Rabbit's miniature bedroom window, I bent and peered into that little wood frame, the paper fraying around its scalloped edge, the little haphazard orchestra set before rows of barracks and untold miles of desert and mountain, a few teenagers and old men gathered beneath a full sepia sun, holding whatever instruments they could scrounge up: a row of girls with violins, men with horns, even a triangle. At the center, framed in the pendant of light from the wine-glass, a boy seated at an upright piano. Just which one is Paul's mother I don't know. I didn't look at their faces, so proud, so undefeated, their clothes so obviously clean and pressed. I thought instead of the music they made in that god-awful camp, the joy of their strings so pathetically hopeful, reminders of the world still raging outside, while at night the sandstorms patrolled their bunks like the foot of God. Did the others dance while they played? In the desert night, who else would have heard them but the ones who shared their detainment?

When I had called Elizabeth from the hospital, she had said, Ah God, so our Paul is gone. And I'd thought, Yes, our Paul. Now we are both widows.

***

The mourning color of the Chinese is white. In Taiwan, because there is so little land, the dead are buried in the mountain where the family burns gold paper and incense and sweeps the grave when a new baby is born or a child is married. Then the family lays out a picnic and eats with the dead. In Korea, the mourners take to the streets and bang loudly. When that's all over, they feast. In the Philippines, a mass is said. Then they feast. In San Francisco, however, the widow takes to drink. A glass of Beaujolais, maybe, in the afternoon. Then he fills the hours till night at the window, wondering if he should water the brown things in the garden or leave them for the wind to tear up. Mourning is like unemployment: the longer one does it, the more reluctant one becomes to reenter the world ouside. The heart, meanwhile, grieves. Which is something totally different.

September.

Elizabeth knocks at the door with groceries. It's four in the afternoon. She appraises my tousled hair and bathrobe and walks into the house without a word and begins to stock the fridge. She washes the pans, clears the soup cans and cardboard trays from the counter, arranges the empty med bottles in a neat row, then steeps two handfuls of ramen in a pot of boiling water. Without a word. Not even so much as a look. Just the jingling of her bracelets. But I'm rattling on nervously, about my publisher pushing me for a deadline, about donating Paul's clothes, about how this house never sees sunlight even in summer. What I really want to say is, just go the hell away. Paul's dead. You have no more business in this house.

She lifts her eyes finally and considers me a moment before cracking an onion in two. As fog descends on the house, we eat silently in the kitchen, our chopsticks chattering against the bowls in our hands.

After she leaves, I shift through the pile of CDs under the stereo for Nina.

Paul and I bought CDs religiously. They were our calendars, the chronicle of our years together, soundtracks of our best and saddest times. That's how we coped: each time someone died, each time someone managed to sign off disability, each time Paul emerged from the hospital only a little bit more ragged, we had an excuse to buy a CD. Every title was an early death, or a life recovered, even if on loan.

Paul had bad taste. He liked European techno and long, drawn-out operas. Trash and pretense. My one clear victory was his conversion to Nina Simone. Paul admitted for once my impeccable nose for good fuck-tracks. For years we humped to Nina carrying grandly through the house. In summer, laying nude at dusk, my face in his neck, feeling no need to do more: *Love me love me love me, say you do-*

I go through the pile of CDs again and again, but no Nina.

Where could it have gone?

***

Ah, God. So our Paul is gone.

Tell me, what did you see? Did you see his spirit lift and follow the others into the sky?

Paul used to follow me into the garden to plant the spring flower beds, his hands fisted around my apron strings. He would squat and talk to me as I worked.

Next week I'll plant daffodils. It'll be spring by then. It'll be spring, and then it'll be summer again.

Wait. Not yet. Let me take off my sweater.

Don't do that. Leave the light off.

Shh. Listen. It's that bird I brought you.

Once, in the garden, Paul squatted next to me with a diagram of a family tree he was working on for school. The tree was nestled with little crayon birds, each one someone in the family. There weren't very many birds. Paul traced with his finger the orange line that crooked down the green shaggy tree. "That one's Daddy, that's you, and there's me."

I looked a second at the triangle of birds he pointed to. "That's very nice, Paolo."

He frowned. "Paolo? Who's Paolo?"

I didn't realize the mistake till he asked. Freudian slip. I smiled and dusted my hands of the fine seeds and pretended to shield my face from the sun. "No one," I told him. "No one."

I lied. Who's Paolo? I waited for him to ask me again, then I would have told him. It was long ago, I would have told him. A summer very long ago. But he never did ask.

How about you? You want to hear a story?

Come and put your head here.

It was long ago. A summer very long ago.

Momma was bedridden that whole summer-

***

October.

I used to promise every summer I would quit smoking by autumn.

Paul once said the primary emotional relationship of my life was with my cigarettes.

This morning I couldn't find the ashtray. I think Elizabeth swiped it. She took the liberty to "clean" the house yesterday, distracting me with her little I'm Dusting routine while really she's sifting through drawers and bedclothes. That pair of Paul's ceramic piglets disappeared some weeks ago. By the time I noticed I had already forgiven her for the theft; the artifacts of a person become finite in death. As she sees it, the estate should be shared, and a mother's rights precede, I suppose, my rights. I think she believes Paul and I were a mathematical oversight: What we should have been is three people.

Which doesn't go very far toward explaining the ashtray. After she cleaned, we took the lawn chairs from under the bed and sat and smoked on the front porch, her drags long and few between, her mouth nodding at the neighbor's children walking barefoot to the their cars, the twilight turning into streetlight, a time for ecstatic contemplation.

In the mirror I watch myself smoke, but it's Elizabeth I see, the lines of her mouth gathering around the stem of the cigarette, a pink pucker drawing, then relaxing. Hot mama.

***

Momma was bedridden that whole summer.

It was two years after the war, and Papa, who'd been an engineer, who'd designed earthquake-proof bridges, found work as a supervisor at a shoe plant by the wharf. Mostly Japanese workers, old and young. Whoever they were before the war, everyone was starting over. Coming back from the camps, we found our homes had been raided. Behind a neighbor's gate, I saw my own bike tethered like a hostage.

One evening Papa brought home a young man whose family had shared our barracks in the camp. We stood awkwardly in the small living room where I slept. I could hear Momma breathing in her room. "Lizzie," Papa said. "You remember who this is, don't you?"

Yes. The Filipino boy, we'd called him. The women in the laundry detail had said that his mother was Filipino and didn't have to follow her husband and her son into the camps but of course she did. That poor woman, they'd said, but what a beautiful son. I'd pretend I was asleep at night and watch him comb his mother's hair on the bed across the aisle. Sometimes he played jazz piano on an old upright in the cafeteria during mess hall duty and some of the women would wipe their hands on their aprons and clap along. Otherwise, he was quiet. When the entertainment committee posted auditions for an orchestra, we both signed up.

I bowed. "Hello again, Paolo."

While I portioned tea into three cups, Papa explained that Paolo's parents had moved east after the war, but he alone decided to come back to San Francisco. Papa got him a job at the shoe plant: "We have to take care of him," Papa announced. Paolo looked steadily into his cup. "And he's going to drive Momma's doctor here on Saturday mornings." Papa clapped a hand on Paolo's neck. "So say 'thank you.'"

From the next weekend on, Paolo would come in with the doctor and wait in the living room while I woke Momma and propped her on a pillow and told Doctor Yamashiro about all the coughing and the color of phlegm Momma was throwing up. For weeks Paolo never spoke, just sat by the front door with a kettle of tea next to him. I would sit with him silently while the doctor talked to Papa in the kitchen. It was never good news that summer. Momma was so far gone she couldn't speak. You could tell she wanted to, though. You could tell she had waited hours for me or Papa just so she could say something. But there it was when she opened her mouth, this eerie hollowness.

One day I rode back with Paolo to the doctor's office for some medicine and after that we were lovers.

***

Paul had a beautiful curved cock, darker than the rest of him, which is saying a lot. Nights when I couldn't sleep I'd slip a hand under his pajama strings and roll that heavy flesh across my fingers, knead the weight of his generous balls until I dozed off, reassured he was still with me. In the old days we fucked each other delirious with our tongues, lost ourselves for weeks in each other's caves, emerged back into consciousness dazed and embarrassed. Both of us were blessed with perfectly bald assholes, a genetic rarity we discovered and buried night after night. Any further penetration we never cared for, maybe tried a few times because it was Christmas or summer solstice. Anal sex reminded us both of white porn, and thoughts of white boys fucking, to put it politely, made us limp.

Until the final lean year, Paul's body was plump, cool between the breasts. His nipples firm as oak shoots, his skin dark as sap. I'd fold my fawn legs between his and lower my face to his body and set out with my tongue to crisscross the whole bare continent of his back; my tongue, connoisseur of his skin's local flavor. The spice-tinged lower nape. That fecund delta at the mouth of his salt-flecked spine. Dairy trough. Egg-washed cheeks. Paul's body was poetry: fat brown poetry.

Philip Huang

Paul's body was vulgar: fat brown sex. First time I saw him at a New Year's Party, I followed the jugs of his butt down one hall and up another, followed semi-hard and half-drunk on the fantasy of his cleaved ass. One thing about Paul: He could stuff a pair of jeans, denim barely holding together across the crotch when he sat, his sex bunched to the left of the tired seam. I never understood what he saw in me, all vertical limbs, lean and taut with grotesque muscle, poverty and famine. I read in his body the language of surplus and reassurance: There is enough, sweetheart. Never again will there be hunger. Eat. Eat.

Then the first wave of lung infections, and the pounds of lovely flesh shed like hair. We'd heard the stories. Wai-Wai had died of it, horrible consumption, the body and its criminal excess boiled away along the mule ride to death. For months, though his mother and I fed him in rounds, I watched Paul's ribs and spine surface from his body like the first spires of a lost city rising from seawater. Then the sores settled like butterflies, paper flowers pinned to his skin. In stable periods, when we bought time with pharmaceutical inundation, the body returned to us was always a little more whittled.

He would wait on the bed for me after I had undressed him, looking apologetically at his own toes, wistful for his old body. Our lovemaking became memorial, our bodies moving according to their own memory, rehearsing again and again the same careful movements our younger selves had choreographed. Nipples, the mound of his tummy, eddies of hair and down, not moving until his cock was wrapped in my tongue, the swell then fish-like thrashing, tissue and teeth and veins. And I never used a condom, not ever. "What are you trying to prove?" Paul would ask. He'd turn out his needle-pocked forearms and hold them toward me: "Take a good look. Don't you see what this has done to me? Well, I'm not going to be the one to do it to you. I won't." But I only locked my head in his crotch until his sentences ran into moans. He wasn't strong enough to argue.

What damn did I give about transmission, about how many viral particles per million particles of clear bitter discharge I swallowed? Because the terrible had happened. The earth had flooded again. The world was in flames. Blow jobs were our acre of dry land, our pocket of air, as if his glans were the knob of a secret door to safety, to a place of cures, if only I could get a good enough grip. Every part of our life had been reduced to archives. I was our last defense, the last line of archery. Here, here and no more. Nothing else will be taken from us.

But I had nothing to save my Paul from the brainfevers. As summer came, the first weeks without rain, Paul began to go mad. His hands would climb the air in sleep, thumb to pinkie, thumb to pinkie, measuring the horse from hooves to ears, over and over again. Sixteen, seventeen. Eighteen hands. My Paul died riding the back of dementia.

One night in July as I lay beside him and held him through a fever, he woke suddenly and looked at me a full minute, deadpan. I searched his face but he wasn't there, and the only word that came to my mind was hush. Hush. I was telling myself. Finally his eyes filled in as if he recognized me and he said, "No promises, OK? No promises." I had laughed, then sat up and cried. It was what I had said to him one morning long ago-in fact the first morning of the new decade- said diplomatically as I rose from his bed, no idea of the years ahead of us both. "No promises, OK?"

Back then he had laughed, too. It was how I had ended our first date.

***

One day I rode back with Paolo and after that we were lovers.

You think I've always been an old woman? You think I don't know what it's like to have boys, good-looking boys, sniffing after me? Paolo had lacquered midnight blue hair. We made love in his room in the Tenderloin. A single room with a sink and a birdcage and long halls of children and old people who couldn't work anymore. The bird would jump around on its perch noisily, trying to get a good view of my legs thrown over its owner's shoulders, my hands gripping the bottom of the tiny cot. We learned to throw a shirt over the cage.

By then I'd already been with two boys, both of whom I didn't care too much about; one smoked cigarettes and the other had a tattoo. I was probably a whore. None of my girlfriends cared; they slept with white men. Paolo smoked but he didn't have any tattoos; just two tiny moles low on his pelvis, dark brown on brown. Umbrae. Penumbrae. Loops of black pubic hair like wildfire corona: He never wore underwear. And that mouth of his. Perpetual pout. One lip like the prow of a ship. The other lip a jelly roll.

He had thick hands, too, but they were always very soft on me. I was only the second girl he'd been with, and if she hadn't begged him to pull her hair and bruise her breasts and make her cuss, then I sure wasn't going to be the first.

After we drove Momma's doctor home, we would buy a pack

of smokes and drive for hours, just drive, anywhere. Where could we go? North, into Marin, the highway rounding the bay like the lip of a glass. I'd hang my arm out the window, feeling the wind fill my palm, like flying, my other hand resting between Paolo's thighs.

Then we would go back to his room and work the day's heat into each other's bodies. By evening I had to be home to cook dinner for Papa. The three of us would eat at the card table in the kitchen, Momma asleep in her room, Paolo and Papa on either side of me, always without a word. Papa was never a talkative man, but that summer, it was like Momma's muteness had infected him, too. Momma was all the woman he ever knew, and she was dying in the next room, on the bed where they slept like spoons in a drawer.

After dinner, Papa would leave to go to his card games and Paolo and I would clear the table and then get together very hush-hush in the bathroom while Momma slept. It always began that way, against the sink, his head under my skirt, his tongue prodding my sex through the cotton of my panties, a finger curling underneath and rubbing for an entrance. Then eating me long and hard, rolling me over the palm of his tongue, the finger going deeper, his other hand fisted around himself. Then the plunge, the plunge-plunge until springs burst into my throat, burst, sweet, shudder and muffled scream, and after I would smoke and watch him wipe himself off and dress.

We never talked much about the future, but once he did say he would take me to someplace that snowed.

Did I love him?

Oh, who's to say?

The last time we made love I looked at his head bent studiously over my breasts as if over a piano and I felt such love for him I couldn't speak. Like Momma. It had swept my body unknown and by the time I noticed, I was too mute to yell for help. Do you know what that's like? Even now, after so many years, I couldn't say why it was exactly we stopped doing what we were doing. Sometimes two people have no more reason for coming apart than they did getting together to begin with. Momma died one Sunday in September and after that I just didn't see Paolo anymore.

I heard he moved to Hawaii a few years later.

***

It's November. I know it's November because someone on the news tonight said it was November. When I look out the window I see, in fact, the trees are a little more bare.

I once saw a picture in one of Paul's abnormal psychology textbooks of two children clinging to each other on a bare floor like two little monkeys. "That's so sad," I'd said. "What's wrong with them?" Paul told me those children were in an abuse shelter. They were comforting each other. For some reason I had taken Paul's face into my hand and kissed him. A month later he came down with a cold that took him out for two weeks.

I never gave it a thought. It was just a cold. No big deal.

I would bring a mug of tea to the bed and he'd sit up and rub his nose and smile at me. I'd actually thought how peaceful we were together, how domestic, my hand feeling for a temperature on Paul's forehead, the toilet grumbling to itself like usual.

Some of our friends were coming down with colds at about the same time, for two or three weeks at a time. "Yeah," I'd tell them on the phone. "Paul's sick, too." It was going around, I'd tell myself.

Can you call it denial? Sometimes I get so angry at myself for not seeing what was happening. Maybe I could've saved him. But life was so good. We had our house. We came home and found each other. It was just a cold. It was going around.

This morning I made a pile of Paul's shirts and curled into it like a little monkey.

When Elizabeth knocked at noon, I pretended I wasn't there at all. Just not at all.

***

I heard Paolo moved to Hawaii a few years later.

Two summers later I was married. What's to tell? A nice enough man asked and I said yes. Papa sat in the front pew and cried.

The first seven years of my marriage I miscarried twice. I carried that second child all the way to his sixth month. Twice my womb opened to the river, dangled its bait in the water, waited for months to see the stem and pink lobe bob into sight. But twice that peach drifted further downstream, into the love of some other woman. My third pregnancy, though, I knew. River calm with certainty. The giant peach washed onto my shore, split open-

And out came a child.

***

I used to fear certain paintings as a child, especially portraits, their eyes following me around the room as if they had something personal to settle with me. I've come to fear Nina Simone's voice in the same way. She knows too much. She knows me.

Paul, would you call that deep paranoia or just melancholy?

I think about Nina in all those Paris psych wards she checked herself into, all those empty white rooms and the bouquets and bouquets of long stems meant for her drooping at the nurses' station, and how she would sit night after night alone listening to the attendants gossip in French just outside her door. Because she takes it just like a woman.

Nina lost in Juarez. Nina at the Village Gate. I listen to her, Paul, and it's you I hear: *I loves you, Porgy. If you can keep me, I wanna stay here with you forever And I'll be glad.*

Last night I watched the neighbors across the street string lights on their garage door. Long after they were finished, I sat in the window and picked at a hole in my sweater and watched the lights circle round and round like a stream of blood.

How could you just leave me? How could you be so selfish, Paul, so damned selfish?

This morning I had a dream that made me ache.

In my dream, you and I are in a hollowed-out military hanger.

Nina steps onto a crate and begins to sing from someplace deep in her throat and I nudge my face into your neck and that is how we dance. We forget the two sad teenage guards smoking in the doorway, the ribbons of black iron fence that keep us from fleeing into the desert on their horses. It becomes a marathon to see who drops first, you or me. Never mind. Never mind. Go ahead and dance. So much, so much of the world falling black and you are touching me and holding me and holding me and that is enough.

Then the sound of metal hitting metal-clank!-and you faded back into white.

I woke to the sound of water sloshing in the sink. Your mother was in the kitchen making lunch, slamming pots on the burners, her way of waking me. She was making noise as if she were jealous, as if she sensed you and I were together again in my dream. As if she would not allow even that. I turned in the bed and looked at the weak, watery sunlight picking through the curtain and waited for her voice.

Your mother: I don't know how she does it, what she tells herself to keep going like she does. She keeps coming around. Why? She never liked me. Never. But she keeps after me, every day, letting herself in, cooking and cleaning and washing clothes. Maybe a mother is just a set of deeply ingrained behaviors that have to be acted out. Maybe the child is just a stimulus. Interchangeable. You're the psychiatrist. You tell me.

***

And out came this perfect child.

Tugged at my breasts, warm wet gums on my nipples. Two dark spots low on the pelvis. There are oracles that must be respected. Paolo. Paolo. Paul.

My husband died seven years later.

It just happens that way; one day you're a little girl, and another day you're a widow with a child tugging at your skirt. You wake up and it could be any year in your life but it happens to be this one. Even the husband you did not love will leave you. I was just one woman. So I held on to my Paul, sealed the world from us, and there we remained for all his childhood, as mother and son, woman and man.

Whenever I called my son's name, it would harken back to me the other young man of the same name, and the years would reel back, the breeze of summer in my hair and the sound of wheels beneath us as we rounded the bay, Saturday, July, August, my hand on top of his hand on top of my knee-

***

Every spring the house fills with strange hungry chirps and flutters from deep in the walls. A family of birds tucked in the ceiling above the bed. Nights when Paul had to stay awake to take his meds, he'd fold his hands together on top of his knees and stare up dreamily and listen to pass the time. Come autumn, the chicks that manage to live fly off someplace warm, leaving the dead ones behind.

I came home one day from the pharmacy to find Paul sitting sheepishly on the bed, his pajamas soaked with urine. I was used to it, but I felt angry suddenly. Just stop this, just stop, I thought. I pulled off his clothes to rinse in the bathtub and rubbed his body roughly with a damp towel. The towel came away pink with the pus from his sores. He didn't complain but hid his face against my chest. Later that night he slept deeply, for once not struggling to breathe, not sweating from the effort of holding still. I sat in the dark, exhausted, but not daring to sleep. I sat absorbing the peace, the tiny flutter of wings overhead lulling me. In the morning, I couldn't wake Paul. I called Elizabeth. That afternoon he was in the hospital and four days later he died.

The senses remember more than the mind. Certain triggers, like a smell or a sound, can bring bubbling to the surface entire undercurrents of memory, a different species of memory than the conscious mind is capable of. Nights still, though it's winter and the birds are long gone, I hear the beating of wings echoing through the walls and it rushes back to me, a sense of peace so deep and perfect that it presses the skin.

***

His hand on top of my hand on top of my knee.

Once I saw a movie where a woman said: "Sure is a shame to have only one man in your life who knew your worth." In my life, I had two. My son, my beautiful boy.

I'll tell you something else, too: He loved you. My son loved you. He'd asked me to take care of you after he died, to treat you as if you were my own flesh and blood. He held my hand as he told me this. He wanted me to promise.

Do you think he's here now?

Next week I'll plant the garden. You can help. It's March already. We can have daffodils.

No, leave your finger where it is. Look what we've done. Some more. I don't want to talk anymore.

***

January.

Of all things, Elizabeth brings me a bird. A fat little thing no bigger than a pack of cigarettes. As she hangs the cage over the dining table she reels off instructions, feeding schedules. Change the lining once a week. Change the water twice a week. If I can't take care of myself I should at least care for another, a dependent life. It's a gap in logic I don't find amusing.

She eyes the shirt I'm wearing, a blue flannel she'd given to Paul from her husband's wardrobe. Paul used to reach for it first thing on a cold morning. I can feel the worn spots on the elbows where he'd rub himself waiting for the shower to run hot.

Elizabeth pulls rings off her fingers and rolls up her sleeves.

"It's too big for you," she says.

All of a sudden I find everything very amusing.

She pulls out bottles of cleaning agents from the reservoir she's stocked under the kitchen sink. Tactfully she rearranges the pile of unpaid, even unopened, bills on the counter without comment. I make a show of sponging off the refrigerator door, where pictures of Paul had been removed in a bold moment of clarity the week before. She moves to the living room, then the bathroom. Scrubbing the blubbery white of the sink, she hums softly to herself, her eyebrows marking the crescendo. Before she leaves she floats a fat gardenia in a bowl of water over the toilet.

This is Paul's true grave, these rooms where he breathed and fucked and died. We both understand that.

I draw a bath. Steam fills the bathroom, infused with the gardenia. I slide into the water. I close my eyes at the first red boils spreading down my thighs. How much longer till they break through? From the bedroom, Nina sings, and in the dining room, the bird begins its own song. In my mind, I form the lines of Elizabeth's face. That's what Paul's face would have looked like, in twenty years, thirty—

Me and her, we're the end of something.

My eyes are closed. The drum sounds like hooves dropping, one, then another, then another—

In the water, my fists begin to open.

from *Rrrrrr:* *Rolling the R's*

R. Zamora Linmark

Salt

The Men's Public Restroom: Ala Moana Beach Park: Late afternoon. One side of the open-shower area is deserted; the stone benches, unoccupied, dry. On the other side: Transistor radio blares out "Babe" by Styx. Edgar is on his back, tanning to Bain de Soleil. Water streams from a shower head, and dives into Vicente's mouth. Standing like a fountain statue, Vicente adjusts the shower knob. Water bullets down to massage his scalp, his neck, his face; to pellet his brows and sting his lips.

A surfer-looking teen clutching a Morey boogie board appears through the veil of water. Tall, muscle-toned, with a rippling stomach, the surfer looks like a local version of Sylvester Stallone with his Rocky Balboa eyes and lips. Vicente turns the shower off.

Edgar cocks an eyebrow as he catches Vicente's eyes trailing after the surfer who, dripping wet, drops his boogie board on the stone bench next to Edgar's. Edgar quickly reaches down for the duffle bag beside him and fishes out a pair of sunglasses while his eyes remain fixed at the surfer's back. Behind dark lenses, Edgar smirks as his mind experiences a deja vu: Edgar, on the toilet, trying hard to pee while his naked father blow-dried his hair.

Turning down the volume of the radio, Edgar asks the surfer: "Wen' catch any big waves?"

"Nah, small the waves over here," the surfer replies.

"So where you go for surf and boogie board?"

"Normally, I go North Shore."

"You mean like Banzai Pipeline?"

"Yeah, over there and Sunset." The surfer pauses. "Why, you surf?"

"Nah, I just watch the waves," Edgar says, then points to Vicente. "My friend over there bodysurfs. His cousin one professional surfer."

"Who?" the surfer asks.

"Michael Ho."

"For real?"

"For real. Go ask him if you no believe."

The surfer turns his head to Vicente and catches him staring. "Go," Edgar nags, "Go ask him if you no believe."

As the surfer saunters toward him, Vicente turns around and grabs the shower knob. Water bites into his face. From behind he can feel Edgar's eyes watching him bend his head down as the surfer, smelling of salt, stands next to him.

"Eh, you Michael Ho's cousin?" the surfer asks.

Vicente's heart pounds hard and fast as the surfer asks again, "So you Michael Ho's cousin or what?"

Vicente rubs his eyes with the heel of his palms to blot out the image of the surfer's firm chest, his taut midriff, his pearl-deep navel, and the hairs peeping out of his Lightning Bolt shorts.

"Eh, you deaf or what," the surfer says, then looks over his shoulder at Edgar, who sits up on the bench, watching while he applies suntan lotion on his thighs.

"He no can hear you," Edgar says, crossing his legs to hide his erection. "The water too loud, that's why."

The surfer moves closer to Vicente, who has cupped his hands over his ears and squeezed his eyes shut. "So what, brah, you Michael Ho's cousin or what?"

Vicente's heart pounds harder and faster as the heat of the surfer's breath penetrates the water around him. He bolts out of the shower but slips, his left arm brushing against the surfer's right leg.

"Eh," the surfer shouts out as Vicente disappears behind the wall.

Edgar throws his belongings into the duffel bag and sprints after Vicente. "Vicente, dumbass, you forgot your towel," he shouts, then mumbles under his breath, "Shit, that surfer was one fresh and easy catch, too." Then, "Vicente, shit, wait for me." But Vicente doesn't hear him. With the imprint of the surfer's skin still smoldering, Vicente races toward the ocean, like lava rushing home.

The Secret

Edgar thinks it's a secret. He thinks it's a secret because Mr. Campos, the custodian, always tells him that no one else can find out. He thinks no one else can find out because by the time he walks into the janitor's room, everyone has already left the school. Everyone except him and Mr. Campos, who sits on the bench next to the mop stand, waiting with his shirt off and his zipper undone.

Edgar thinks it's a secret because each time Mr. Campos signals him to take off his shirt from Kress or his Toughskin pants from Sears or his rubber shoes from Thom McAn, only he answers to his silent calls. He thinks it's a secret because only he and Mr. Campos know they have just half an hour before the shirt, pants, and shoes must be put on again. He thinks it's a secret because he never sees Mr. Campos' son, who comes to pick Mr. Campos up every day.

Edgar thinks it's a secret when Mr. Campos tells him to lie flat on his stomach or on his back, because only he feels the words. He thinks it's a secret no one can ever find out because it is only his lips and no one else's that Mr. Campos wets, or it is only his neck and no one else's that Mr. Campos licks then blows, or it is only his chest and no one else's that Mr. Campos kisses.

Edgar thinks it's a secret because only he can feel the graying hair brushing against his skin. His skin and no one else's.

Edgar thinks it's a secret Mr. Campos must keep for the rest of his life because Mr. Campos can never tell his wife how Edgar lies flat on his stomach or on his back and runs his tongue on Mr. Campos' cracked lips or licks then blows his neck or kisses his hairless chest.

Edgar thinks it's a secret Mr. Campos can never tell his wife because only Mr. Campos can feel the child's hair, fine as silk, brushing against him. Only he can feel the rejuvenation because only Edgar can feel the white hairs pricking his face.

Edgar thinks it's a secret when Mr. Campos buries his face between Edgar's legs because only he can feel his own heart beating louder and louder as Edgar raises his feet higher and higher. Edgar thinks it's a secret because only he can feel his feet stiffening, his small toes curling. Edgar thinks it's a secret Mr.

Campos can never tell because it is forever buried in his mouth, alive and young.

Edgar thinks it's a secret when Mr. Campos, not being able to hold it in, shoots all over him and groans loud enough for the walls to hear.

Edgar thinks it's a secret despite the loud groans. He thinks it's a secret because, though the walls hear him, the walls don't have mouths. He thinks it's a secret because the sound does not escape the room, but echoes again and again in their sighing kisses.

Edgar thinks it's a secret because, though he has to wipe himself with his own shirt, he can always soak it with soap and Clorox as soon as he gets home. He thinks it's a secret because no matter how many times he tries to scrub his body, the smell of Mr. Campos is forever buried in his skin.

Mr. Campos thinks it's still a secret between him and Edgar when Edgar tells Vicente about it. He thinks it's a secret because, before Edgar walks into the janitor's room, he does not hear Edgar telling Vicente to wait until the green door is shut. It's a secret Mr. Campos can never find out because he does not see Vicente watching him through the keyhole. Watching Mr. Campos as he waits on the bench next to the mop stand with his shirt off and his zipper down.

Mr. Campos thinks it's a secret between him and Edgar because he does not see Vicente's eyes each time he signals Edgar to take off his clothes. He thinks only Edgar answers to his silent calls. He thinks only he and Edgar know about the thirty-minute rendezvous.

Mr. Campos thinks it's a secret because he does not know

Vicente can hear his faint voice telling Edgar to lie flat on his stomach or on his back. He does not see Vicente's eyes opening wide when he buries his face between Edgar's legs. Vicente's eyes getting wider and wider as Edgar's legs rise higher and higher until toes curl in the air.

Mr. Campos thinks it's a secret when, not being able to hold it in, he shoots all over Edgar and groans. He thinks it's a secret despite the loud groans because, though the walls hear him, the walls don't have mouths. He does not know that, though the walls don't have mouths, the door has eyes.

Mr. Campos thinks it's a secret because he does not see Vicente watching Edgar wipe himself with his own shirt that he soaks with soap and Clorox as soon as he gets home. Mr. Campos thinks it's a secret because he does not see Edgar reaching his arms out and telling Vicente to smell the secret that Mr. Campos thinks is forever buried in his skin.

night sweats

Joël B. Tan

for joey, again and again and again

Even now, I remember the sweat between us. I can smell our lovemaking, a mixture of cologne, lube, saliva and sweat. I can feel him, heavy on my chest. I can taste the lubricant, his kisses, our perspiration...and the sweet taste of his semen. Manolo was my first love.

Southwest Airlines, the great big bus in the sky, landed before it had the chance to reach the full climax of flight. Burbank to San Diego was a short trip and I had to weigh cost and purpose when deciding whether to fly for half an hour or drive for two and a half. But this was an emergency.

My dreams of Manolo are memories.

Nothing could have prepared my twenty-year-old heart for what I've been through with this man that I met almost ten years ago. Watching Manolo move was like watching porn—the motherfucker was that fine. Most times, it was unbearable to walk down the street with him because his curly mestizo hair and slanted eyes, his body as thick and threatening as a fist prompted licked lips and double takes from strangers. He walked with a certain style; arms swung like metronomes, fists clenched. He was regimented, choreographed, controlled. He often reminded me of a soldier or a pugilist, proud and afraid, as if going into battle or the ring.

From go, I knew fucking was inevitable. It was something about the way we danced together. I've always believed that you can tell how a person fucks by the way they dance. We attributed our rhythm to our island ancestry and the drum magic that flowed in our blood. Manolo was Puerto Rican. I am Pilipino. Given all the Roman Catholic, Spanish-colonized baggage we both carried, we were doomed. Nevertheless, we fell in love.

We were extreme opposites. I am openly gay. Manolo was into the straight acting, straight appearing, macho posturing. He enjoyed the nightclub frenzy of Friday nights while I preferred the lazy warm comforts of Sunday mornings. I was a book fiend; Manolo, a TV junkie. He was a troubled but practicing Catholic. I preferred a generic spirituality that bucked convention and institutions. I was the talker; Manolo was often quiet and moody.

Manolo and I fucked a lot. Although we were clearly incompatible, we compensated by devouring each other's bodies. We never really learned how to talk to one another since a sharing of opinions would quickly turn into arguments. Rather than engage in the futile exercise of conversation, we made our bodies the primary instrument of communication. We articulated feelings with our kisses. We probed with our tongues. We expressed joy with our fingers. We resolved our differences with our cocks. It got to be so that we could express grief, sorrow, anger, fraternity, empathy, sympathy, any and every feeling in our lovemaking. At the end of our heavy breathing, we were always silent. In the dark, we would lie on our sweat-soaked sheets, reconciled with our exchange of flesh. We developed a language of our own.

Our bodies fit together perfectly. A brush of the hand would lead to a soft caress. The soft caress would quickly turn into fingers pinching nipples. Twisted nipples would turn into wide canyon kisses. Zippers would fly open, shirts would be flung.

Waistbands of boxers yanked down, knife-like tongue on Adam's apple, teeth gnashing delicate corners, ring fingers probing, cocks hard.

We weren't much for slow, gentle exchanges. In fact, we fucked with the ferocity of a brutal joust. We would grunt, yell, scream, kick, bite, taunt, and push. Our mating habits invoked notions of prescience. If anybody had heard us, they would probably have thought we were trying to kill each other. Most times, fucking and fighting became the same thing, but at the apex of his orgasms, Manolo would yell, "I love you" or "*Te amo*" (as if surrendering). When we had milked our last drop, he would engulf my body with kisses as soft and tender as a child's. In return, I too would surrender and confess: "*Mahal kita.* I love you, Manolo. *Mahal kita.*"

Our beginning was as doomed as it was exhilarating. We were both young and handsome. We needed to be needed. Mistaking mind-blowing sex for a divine order to cohabitate we moved into a three-bedroom apartment we couldn't really afford, after only a few months of dating.

We created a beautiful home on credit and silences. We littered the house with tasteful antiques, paintings by contemporary Puerto Rican artists, native Pilipino art, and small talk. We created the perfect environment. We fucked in every corner of our large apartment. We christened three bedrooms, two and a half baths, an outdoor patio, a fully equipped kitchen, a formal dining room, and a sunken den with our sweat and semen. We played out our domestic fantasies knowing that we couldn't possibly pay back the debt we'd incurred. When the last stick of furniture was bought, we knew it was over.

Eventually, playing house and having great sex couldn't cut it anymore. As if our differences weren't enough, Manolo had a problem with lying, and it finally broke me, broke us. His best friend once confided that his lying started when he was young. Apparently Manolo's father had a severe drinking problem. They say that he died with a bottle in one hand and a gun in the other. Manolo's father left his mother and his sisters a legacy of violence, disappointment, and brutality, nothing more. Shortly after his death, Manolo's mother buried herself under suicidal mounds of cocaine. What was left of their family soon disintegrated. Manolo never could accept reality as it was, so he fabricated his own.

In retrospect, I realize that my leaving Manolo was inevitable. Nevertheless, the pain of walking away from him was excruciating. He was the first man who ever made me feel needed and loved. Young love like that is never meant to last long.

His absence became a void I desperately tried to fill with drunken Friday nights. I became an indiscriminating receptacle for anyone's attention or affection. I searched for men who resembled him, no matter how slightly. I sought refuge from one man to the next. I was barely breathing.

In a gay community as small as L.A.'s, word always got back to me about Manolo. Mutual friends reported Manolo's stunts-the temper fits, the fights-and each time they did, it took everything I had to resist picking up his midnight answering machine messages, which begged and demanded night after night. He blamed me for abandoning him. He told me that he didn't need me. He couldn't understand why I had left. He thought we were perfect together. Eventually, he stopped calling and I realized that I'd been replaced. He found a convenient and easy solace. He found a medicine that offered him the magic cure for bad feelings and broken hearts. He made his reality happier and higher with his crystal, booze, and whatever else he could snort, shoot, swallow or smoke.

The vices he once rebuked became his salvation. The addicted parents he once disowned came back to haunt him through his own hollow reflection. Manolo's habits demanded more time, so he quit his job before he was asked to leave. He got involved in credit fraud, petty theft, and other types of scams. He quickly learned that his amateurish criminal activity wasn't enough to meet the needs of his bottomless appetite. Crystal and everything else he dropped devoured him. His once heavily-muscled frame caved in, giving way to a thin, jackal-like shadow with sharp teeth and sad eyes. When he had nothing left to sell, he gladly traded his mouth, his cock, his ass for another line, another hit.

I saw him once at a burger shack on Santa Monica and Virgil. He was facing the street, smoking a cigarette to its butt, hunting for prey. He had the rabid look of a professional and his hunger was apparent. When he looked into the intersection and recognized me, he quickly turned his back. After what seemed to be eons, the light turned green and I sped off. Without looking back, I felt his gaze, angry and desperate, drilling a clear message: Stop. Don't leave me.

After that incident, he simply vanished for six years. Without hearing anything else through the grapevine, I just assumed that he was dead. One day, I received a call at work. It was Manolo. He was calling to invite me to his graduation from a drug rehabilitation program. Proudly, he told me that he had finally completed six months of abstinence and sobriety from crystal and alcohol. This was his fourth attempt in this particular program. His counselors assigned him to a transitional house in Oceanside with other recovering addicts as a condition for his parole.

In great detail, he told me his story. He recounted the past six years-needles, fat lines on slick mirrors, dollar wine, more lies, hooking, loan sharks, the old men, jail, rape, the police, suicide attempts, the program, back to selling drugs, doing drugs, five-dollar tricks, robbing, being robbed, the program again, back out, the habit again, hotels, a drug bust, conviction, sentencing, the pen, parole, rehab, and finally, graduation.

With some hesitation, I accepted his invitation. When I arrived I realized that I was his only guest. Six years of rough living had definitely taken its toll. He looked older, weathered. Sobriety and jail yard weights had put about thirty pounds of muscle around his shoulders, chest and arms. He had a slight belly that only added to the menacing bulk of his muscles. His trim beard and shaved head brought out the delicate slant of his eyes and the stubborness of his jaw. The back of his neck and his forearms revealed tattoos in "Olde English" script that hadn't been there in our youth. He looked sinister, menacing. He was even more alluring than I remembered.

To my surprise, he broke from his fellow graduates to hug me. Unabashedly, he planted a wet kiss on my lips. I froze, shocked by both his spontaneous display of affection and my lips' quick return. He drew back, eyes down, apologizing. Before I could react, a group of his friends called him over; the ceremonies were about to begin.

Manolo was among the few from his graduating class to speak. He delivered a painfully honest speech about his journey to recovery. I'd never heard him speak as eloquently and as honestly about his feelings as he did that day. Humble and penitent, he announced that his recovery still depended on his making ammends to people he had loved and hurt. From the stage, his eyes met mine. This both excited me and made me nervous. Was this the same man I had known six years ago?

When the ceremonies were over, we quickly broke from the crowd. I offered Manolo a ride to his new home in Oceanside-a two-hour drive from Los Angeles.

We took the ocean view route along the Pacific. I skimmed over the dull events of the last four years and recounted one failed relationship after another. Keith, Fernando, Greg, Arnel, another Greg, Robert, Magno, Enrique, Keith again; now, I was single. Although I was apprehensive, I asked him if he had any current love interests.

Shaking his head, Manolo flatly announced that he had recently tested HIV-positive. He told me he had been tested a year ago, after suffering from night sweats and other unexplained ailments. Since he had slightly under two hundred T-cells, he had an official diagnosis of AIDS. He attempted to lessen the severity of his announcement by explaining that he was currently on medication and treatments that had greatly diminished his symptoms and he spoke with an optimism that was hard to believe. He suspected that he had probably been infected for some time, but he was glad that the program had been there to help him cope. No one knew; neither his family nor his friends. He confessed that although he saw his diagnosis as the wake-up call that had finally brought him to sobriety, he often felt like a leper. He hadn't been able to touch anybody since his diagnosis, he said. He was afraid of potentially infecting someone. After a long silence, he placed his hand over mine and asked me if I was negative or positive.

I told him that I was negative. And as if I were offering a consolation, I tried to put him at ease by sharing that I was no stranger to HIV. In fact, many of my friends, and a couple of my past lovers, have lived with and some have died from AIDS. "It's all such a crap shoot, isn't it?" I said. He said nothing and just held my hand tighter. A familiar heat seeped through his fingers into mine. Impulsively, I pulled off the freeway and drove up to a roadside Econo-Lodge.

I parked my car, headed toward the office, and asked for a room with a large bed. Manolo seemed confused. I said nothing and simply led him to our designated room. In the dark motel room, I removed my clothes. He said nothing and just watched each article drop to the floor.

Naked, I headed toward him until I found his lips. His hungry tongue probed my mouth as I tugged at his shirt and yanked at his jeans. When he was completely disrobed, I pushed him away. I wanted to drink in the sight of Manolo's nakedness. He was weaving slightly as if he were drunk. A thin film of sweat that covered his heaving body glistened silver-blue from the sunset's dying light. I got on my knees and met his half-hard cock. The dark purple knob was beginning to protrude from its sheath. Without hesitation, I took his quickly stiffening member in my mouth.

"Please! Don't," he begged.

I ignored his pleas and resurrected the beast. Surrendering, he gripped my bobbing head with all his old fury as he started to fuck my mouth. I slid to the floor and offered myself completely. He sat down, bringing down a familiar weight on my chest. Manolo started to rub and tease his saliva-wet prick across my face with the grace of a snake charmer. His hairy thighs scraped roughly under my arms. His cock blocked my airways but I no longer needed air to breathe. We were drenched with the rain of our sweat, precum, and spit. The air was pungent and thick with our union. Releasing myself from his grasp, I climbed aboard the creaky motel bed. I unwrapped a condom, slid it over his gargantuan shaft, and quickly ordered: "Fuck me. Like you used to."

He threw my legs over his shoulders like a harness of flesh as I proceeded to grind my hips closer to the hard heat of his cock. In one confident stroke, he pushed into my waiting chasm without mercy or grace, forcing my tight muscle ring to accommodate beyond its usual capacity. Waves of pain washed across the length of my body. I was drowning in acid sweat and memories. The rhythm claimed us and we remembered our dance. At the end of our intense melee, the words *I love you*, *Te amo*, *Mahal kita*, and tender kisses were exchanged.

We called on our lost language of lovemaking to articulate what we couldn't with words. It became clear to me then. When we were young, we were both unwilling and incapable of negotiating or working through our fears and anxieties. Fate, distance, maturity, recovery, shared pain, and the reality of our impending mortalities afforded us this opportunity to finally establish resolution. We did it in the best way we knew.

He called room service to send up more sheets, but the damage we created was irreparable. We took a shower together. The hot water, his odor mingled with mine, the gentle kisses, the aftermath of our ferocious tangle brought back happy young memories of matrimony. Like children, we washed each other's backs and laughed.

That was the last time I saw Manolo healthy. He landed a job at a local rehab program in San Diego. My writing career demanded more time. He found his niche peer-counseling other HIV-positive addicts. Life events were traded via letters and long-distance calls. Months melted into years and Manolo evolved from remembered childhood lover to an old friend calling with an occasional hello on late nights; or sending funny birthday cards, religious Christmas cards, and oddly enough, anniversary cards.

When I arrived at the hospital, his case manager was there waiting for me. Manolo had never even hinted as to how serious his condition was. He downplayed all his symptoms over the phone. In fact, colds were really bouts of pneumocystis. He was also battling a variety of other opportunistic infections that his immune system was no longer able to resist. Manolo had lied to me again. I was furious.

According to his wishes, Manolo was to be taken off life-support systems at eight A.M. the next morning. His savings covered his crematorial expenses. He had explicitly requested that I be present before he died. Before she politely excused herself, Manolo's caseworker handed me an envelope. Inside was a letter in Manolo's handwriting. The contents read:

Mi Vida,

Please don't be mad. I know you are, but I didn't want to worry you. I guess you wouldn't be surprised if I told you I couldn't find the words to tell you about my condition. Forgive me, for everything. Papa, I will always love you. I will always be with you. Until next time?

Mil besos,,

Manolo Santo.

That night, the nurses, doctors, and caseworkers left me alone with Manolo. AIDS had destroyed his Herculean body. There was nothing left of him but a bare skeletal frame. His breathing was labored, heavy, monitored. His hair clung in thin sorry patches. His unattended beard grew wildly around his hollow cheeks and jaw; still beautiful, still stubborn. His eyelids, paper-thin and veiny, sunk deep into his sockets as if his eyes had retreated or been removed.

His body was a highway of wires and thick plastic tubes. The air-conditioned cold room was filled with the beeping and pulsing sounds of technology and its cruel miracles. A small, dim light came under the crack of the room's closed door. It illuminated his chemotherapy-tanned face, now angelic and grotesque at the same time.

In the darkness of the hospital room, I removed my clothes and headed toward matrimony. I untied the gown that fell easily from my lover's body. He was curled in a fetal position. With great care, I maneuvered my body under the wires, under the tubes, and lay spoon-style with my dying Manolo. My arm slipped easily under his featherweight body as I placed my hand over his weakly beating heart. I protectively wrapped my legs around his bony, jutting hips, burying my face in the wispy patches of his hair. Painstakingly, I pushed his catheter aside and gripped his flaccid penis. In the dark, I rocked him.

His body gave off a cold night sweat, our final baptismal. This would be the last time. My erect penis moved along the rim of his sagging buttocks. That night, I spoke to him. Words were insufficient, so I spoke to him in our primary tongue. I held him tighter, making love to his hollow shell. That night, I buried prayers in his hair. I hid blessings in his mouth. I rubbed his lips with my tears. That night, with one final thrust, I bid Manolo farewell.

When it was over, I dressed him. I took my razor and shaved off his beard. Carefully, I washed his feet and hands and combed his hair. At eight A.M., his doctor and his caseworker arrived with long, regretful faces. I insisted on hitting the switch. I was barely breathing.

Even now, I remember the sweat between us. I can smell our lovemaking, a mixture of cologne, lube, saliva, and sweat. I can feel the heavy weight of him on my chest. I can taste the lubricant, his kisses, our perspiration, and the sweet taste of his semen. Manolo was my first love.

About the Authors

Nino Alvarez is the proud owner of restaurant /club BOMBA in San Juan, Puerto Rico, where he resides with two dogs, two children (Manila and Havana), and his signficant others. "True Love" is his first published fiction.

Justin Chin was born in Malaysia and raised in Singapore. He is the author of *Bite Hard* (Manic D), a collection of poetry and prose. A writer and an artist, he now resides in San Francisco.

Lawrence Chua is the author of *Gold by the Inch* (Grove).

Jaime Cortez is a comedian, illustrator, poet, and photographer. He is the editor of "A La Brava" and an upcoming anthology of queer Latino writing. He lives in San Francisco's Mission District.

Quang H. Dang was born in Vietnam and raised in Alabama, Virginia, and Maryland. His essays have appeared in the *Lesbian and Gay Almanac* in 1996 and he has been published as an anonymous contributor to *Penthouse Forum.* He currently resides in San Francisco's Mission District.

Jay Ruben Dayrit's fiction has appeared in *His 2: Brilliant New Fiction by Gay Writers* (Faber & Faber), *Contemporary Fiction by Filipinos in America* (Anvil), *The Minnesota Review*, *The Santa Clara Review*, *Nexus*, and *Bleach.* He holds a BA in Theatre

Studies from Yale University and an MA in Creative Writing from San Francisco State University. "Our Sunny Afternoon Together" is Jay's only attempt at erotica, and despite what the narrator says, the story is entirely fictional.

Ferd Eggan is a gwm/pwa who works as the AIDS Coordinator of the City of Los Angeles. He has a long history of antiracist activism from the '60s to the present. He also directed and acted in three porn movies: *Billy Rainey's Brother*, *Thongs of Experience*, and *Straight Banana*, and has published many poems and articles, as well as two books, *Your LIFE story by someone else* (Editorial El Coqui) and *Pornography* (Bench Press).

Philip Huang is a recent graduate of the English program at UC Berkeley. This is his first published short story. He thanks Joël B. Tan for his unflinching scrutiny.

Chen Lin was born in Taipei, Taiwan, and raised in Southern California. His work has appeared in various journals and anthologies, including *New to North America: Writings by U.S. Immigrants, Their Children and Grandchildren*, and *RICE: Explorations into Gay Asian Culture and Politics.*

R. Zamora Linmark is the author of *Rolling the R's*. He is currently working on his second novel, *Leche*. He is a 1998 recipient of the Fulbright Scholarship and one of *The Advocate* magazine's list of top promising fifty people under thirty.

About the Authors

Jason Guillermo Luz is a sometime writer/artist. Although his work in the past has comprised mostly poetry *(Maganda Magazine)*, he is interested in writing short fiction and other more narrative forms. This is his first attempt at short story writing.

Dan Taulapapa McMullin is a Samoan writer from Los Angeles, living in San Francisco. His libretti, stories, and plays have been published in *Bamboo Ridge*, *Wasafiri*, *Folauga*, and *Colors*. As a playwright and performer he has been produced at the New Zealand International Arts Festival, the Pacific Festival of Arts in Samoa, Soho Rep in New York, and Theatre Mu in Minneapolis. His play *Sodomie* is under option for film under the title *Bikini Boy*, and he is working on his second full-length play, *The Demon Anchors*.

Allen de Souza is an artist and writer based in LA. His fiction has appeared in *On a Bed of Rice*, *Amerasia Journal*, and *Third Text Journal*. He is the author of *The Sikhs in Britain*.

S'Naughty Spice is a mixed-blood writer and HIV activist.

Andrew Spieldenner (Vietnamese Amerasian) is a community organizer and a longtime HIV activist who resides in NYC. His essays and poems have appeared in *Names We Call Home-Autobiography on Racial Identity* (Routledge), *Voices of Identity, Rage, and Empowerment* (No Press Collective), and the Vietnamese journal *doi dien*.

About the Authors

John Tunui hails from the Royal Family of the Cook Islands, and is a New Zealander now living in San Francisco with his new family. *The Russian Hillbilly*, from which "Liberty" is excerpted, is a chronicle of his childhood on Aitutaki at the time of fallout from nuclear testing, his life as a homeless hustler in the streets of San Francisco, and his time in the bed of a French boy in New York.

"Scents and Sensibility" is **Sonny Alberto Vajrabukka's** third foray into prose. As a senior, he curated an Asian and Pacific Islander Poetry and Performance Series at UCLA (1994-95); he was recently published in *Maganda Magazine* (UC Berkeley).

Virgil Vang is a pseudonym for a popular gay Asian writer.

About the Editor

Joël Barraquiel Tan is an editor, writer, and activist. His essays, short fiction, and poetry can be found in *Asian American Sexualities* (Routledge), *On a Bed of Rice* (Anchor), *Q&A* (Temple), *Blood Whispers: L.A. Poets on AIDS*, and other journals and magazines. Tan is a cofounder of the Asian Pacific AIDS Intervention Team in Los Angeles and has worked with Colors United Action Coalition and Barangay, a Pilipino gay men's organization.

HOT EROTICA FROM CLEIS PRESS!

MORE BOOKS FROM CLEIS PRESS...

DEBUT LITERATURE

The Little School: Tales of Disappearance and Survival, second edition, by Alicia Partnoy.
ISBN: 1-57344-029-9 14.95 paper.

Marianne Faithfull's Cigarette: Poems by Gerry Gomez Pearlberg.
ISBN: 1-57344-034-5 12.95 paper

Memory Mambo by Achy Obejas.
Lambda Literary Award Winner.
ISBN: 1-57344-017-5 12.95 paper.

Queer Dog: Homo Pup Poetry, edited by Gerry Gomez Pearlberg.
ISBN: 1-57344-071-X. 12.95. paper.

We Came All the Way from Cuba So You Could Dress Like This? Stories by Achy Obejas.
Lambda Literary Award Nominee.
ISBN: 0-939416-93-X 10.95 paper.

Seeing Dell by Carol Guess
ISBN: 1-57344-023-X 12.95 paper.

MYSTERIES

Dirty Weekend: A Novel of Revenge by Helen Zahavi.
ISBN: 0-939416-85-9 10.95 paper.

The Woman Who Knew Too Much: A Cordelia Morgan Mystery by B. Reese Johnson.
ISBN: 1-57344-045-0 12.95 paper.

VAMPIRES & HORROR

Brothers of the Night: Gay Vampire Stories, edited by Michael Rowe and Thomas S. Roche.
ISBN: 1-57344-025-6 14.95 paper.

Dark Angels: Lesbian Vampire Stories, edited by Pam Keesey.
Lambda Literary Award Nominee.
ISBN 1-7344-014-0 10.95 paper.

Daughters of Darkness: Lesbian Vampire Stories, second edition, edited by Pam Keesey.
ISBN: 1-57344-076-0 14.95 paper.

Vamps: An Illustrtated History of the Femme Fatale by Pam Keesey.
ISBN: 1-57344-026-4 21.95

Sons of Darkness: Tales of Men, Blood and Immortality, edited by Michael Rowe and Thomas S. Roche. Lambda Literary Award Nominee.
ISBN: 1-57344-059-0 12.95 paper.

Women Who Run with the Werewolves: Tales of Blood, Lust and Metamorphosis,
edited by Pam Keesey. Lambda Literary Award Nominee.
ISBN: 1-57344-057-4 12.95 paper.

SEXUAL POLITICS

Forbidden Passages: Writings Banned in Canada,
introductions by Pat Califia and Janine Fuller. Lambda Literary Award Winner.
ISBN: 1-57344-019-1 14.95 paper.

Public Sex: The Culture of Radical Sex
by Pat Califia.
ISBN: 0-939416-89-1 12.95 paper.

Real Live Nude Girl: Chronicles of Sex-Positive Culture
by Carol Queen.
ISBN: 1-57344-073-6 14.95 paper.

Sex Work: Writings by Women in the Sex Industry, second edition,
edited by Frédérique Delacoste and Priscilla Alexander.
ISBN: 1-57344-042-6 19.95 paper.

Susie Bright's Sexual Reality: A Virtual Sex World Reader
by Susie Bright.
ISBN: 0-939416-59-X 9.95 paper.

Susie Bright's Sexwise
by Susie Bright.
ISBN: 1-57344-002-7 10.95 paper.

Susie Sexpert's Lesbian Sex World,
second edition, by Susie Bright.
ISBN: 1-57344-077-9 14.95 paper.

GENDER TRANSGRESSION

Body Alchemy: Transsexual Portraits
by Loren Cameron.
Lambda Literary Award Winner.
ISBN: 1-57344-062-0 24.95 paper.

Dagger: On Butch Women,
edited by Roxxie, Lily Burana, and Linnea Due.
ISBN: 0-939416-82-4 14.95 paper.

I Am My Own Woman: The Outlaw Life of Charlotte von Mahlsdorf,
translated by Jean Hollander.
ISBN: 1-57344-010-8 12.95 paper.

PoMoSexuals: Challenging Assumptions about Gender and Sexuality ,
edited by Carol Queen and Lawrence Schimel. Preface by Kate Bornstein.
ISBN: 1-57344-074-4 14.95 paper.

Sex Changes: The Politics of Transgenderism
by Pat Califia
ISBN: 1-57344-072-8 16.95 paper.

Switch Hitters: Lesbians Write Gay Male Erotica and Gay Men Write Lesbian Erotica,
edited by Carol Queen and Lawrence Schimel.
ISBN: 1-57344-021-3 12.95 paper.

LESBIAN AND GAY STUDIES

Case of the Good for Nothing Girlfriend: A Nancy Clue Mystery, 2nd edition,
by Mabel Maney.
ISBN: 0-939416-91-3 14.95

The Case of the Not-So-Nice Nurse
by Mabel Maney.
Lambda Literary Award Nominee.
ISBN: 0-939416-76-X 9.95 paper.

Chasing the American Dyke Dream: Homestretch,
edited by Susan Fox Rogers.
ISBN: 1-57344-036-1 14.95 paper.

A Fragile Union: New & Selected Writings
by Joan Nestle.
1-57344-040-X 14.95

Nancy Clue and the Hardly Boys in A Ghost in the Closet
by Mabel Maney. Lambda Literary Award Nominee.
ISBN: 1-57344-012-4 10.95 paper.

Different Daughters: A Book by Mothers of Lesbians,
second edition,
edited by Louise Rafkin.
ISBN: 1-57344-050-7 12.95 paper.

A Lesbian Love Advisor
by Celeste West.
ISBN: 0-939416-26-3 9.95 paper.

On the Rails: A Memoir,
second edition,
by Linda Niemann. Introduction by Leslie Marmon Silko.
ISBN: 1-57344-064-7 14.95 paper.

SEX GUIDES

Good Sex: Real Stories from Real People, second edition,
by Julia Hutton.
ISBN: 1-57344-000-0 14.95 paper.

The New Good Vibrations Guide to Sex: Tips and Techniques from America's Favorite Sex-Toy Store,
second edition, by Cathy Winks and Anne Semans.
ISBN: 1-57344-069-8 21.95 paper.

The Ultimate Guide to Anal Sex for Women by Tristan Taormino.
ISBN: 1-57344-028-0 14.95 paper.

WORLD LITERATURE

A Forbidden Passion
by Cristina Peri Rossi.
ISBN: 0-939416-68-9 9.95 paper.

Half a Revolution: Contemporary Fiction by Russian Women,
edited by Masha Gessen.
ISBN 1-57344-006-X 12.95 paper.

COMIX

Dyke Strippers: Lesbian Cartoonists A to Z,
edited by Roz Warren.
ISBN: 1-57344-008-6 16.95 paper.

TRAVEL & COOKING

Betty and Pansy's Severe Queer Review of New York
by Betty Pearl and Pansy.
ISBN: 1-57344-070-1 10.95 paper.

Betty and Pansy's Severe Queer Review of San Francisco
by Betty Pearl and Pansy.
ISBN: 1-57344-056-6 10.95 paper.

Food for Life & Other Dish,
edited by Lawrence Schimel.
ISBN: 1-57344-061-2 14.95 paper.

WRITER'S REFERENCE

Putting Out: The Essential Publishing Resource Guide for Gay and Lesbian Writers, fourth edition, by Edisol W. Dotson.
ISBN: 1-57344-033-7 14.95 paper.

Since 1980, Cleis Press has published provocative, smart books - for girlfriends of all genders. Cleis Press books are easy to find at your favorite bookstore - or direct from us! We welcome your order and will ship your books as quickly as possible. Individual orders must be prepaid (U.S. dollars only). Please add 15% shipping. CA residents add 8.5% sales tax. MasterCard and Visa orders: include account number, exp. date, and signature.

How to Order

- Phone: 1-800-780-2279 or (415) 575-4700
  Monday - Friday, 9 am - 5 pm Pacific Standard Time
- Fax: (415) 575-4705
- Mail: Cleis Press P.O. Box 14684, San Francisco, California 94114
- E-mail: Cleis@aol.com